"We need to be cautious but not paranoid."

Sarah stepped away from him and reached behind her back to untie her long apron. When she cast aside the pin-striped apron and adjusted the collar on her blouse, Blake was struck by the contrast between the rich teal fabric and her milky skin. A tiny, heart-shaped gold locket nestled in the hollow of her throat.

His fingers itched to caress her, and he actually stuffed his hands into the pockets of his jeans to keep from reaching out and tracing the path of the delicate gold chain that encircled her neck.

As she crossed the kitchen to hang her apron on a peg near the door, he watched her athletic stride and unconsciously graceful gestures.

Being alone with her might be a mistake.

If so, it was an error in judgment he intended to make repeatedly.

SNOWED IN

USA TODAY Bestselling Author

CASSIE MILES

To Kersten Bergstrom and Sonny Caporale with congratulations and hopes for a wonderful life together. And, as always, to Rick.

ISBN-13: 978-0-373-74802-0

SNOWED IN

This edition published by arrangement with Harlequin Books S.A.

For questions and comments about the quality of this book, please contact us at CustomerService@Harlequin.com.

Printed in U.S.A.

ABOUT THE AUTHOR

Though born in Chicago and raised in L.A., *USA TODAY* bestselling author Cassie Miles has lived in Colorado long enough to be considered a semi-native. The first home she owned was a log cabin in the mountains overlooking Elk Creek, with a thirty-mile commute to her work at the *Denver Post*.

After raising two daughters and cooking tons of macaroni and cheese for her family, Cassie is trying to be more adventurous in her culinary efforts. Ceviche, anyone? She's discovered that almost anything tastes better with wine. When she's not plotting Harlequin Intrigue books, Cassie likes to hang out at the Denver Botanical Gardens near her high-rise home.

Books by Cassie Miles

HARLEQUIN INTRIGUE

904—UNDERCOVER COLORADO**
910—MURDER ON THE MOUNTAIN**
948—FOOTPRINTS IN THE SNOW
978—PROTECTIVE CONFINEMENT*
984—COMPROMISED SECURITY*
999—NAVAJO ECHOES
1025—CHRISTMAS COVER-UP
1048—MYSTERIOUS MILLIONAIRE
1074—IN THE MANOR WITH THE MILLIONAIRE
1102—CHRISTMAS CRIME IN COLORADO
1126—CRIMINALLY HANDSOME
1165—COLORADO ABDUCTION#
1171—BODYGUARD UNDER THE MISTLETOE‡
1177—SECLUDED WITH THE COWBOY‡
1193—INDESTRUCTIBLE
1223—LOCK, STOCK AND SECRET BABY§§
1229—HOOK, LINE AND SHOTGUN BRIDE§§
1255—MOUNTAIN MIDWIFE
1279—UNFORGETTABLE
1293—SOVEREIGN SHERIFF
1317—BABY BATTALION
1343—MIDWIFE COVER
1368—MOMMY MIDWIFE
1384—MONTANA MIDWIFE
1402—HOSTAGE MIDWIFE
1454—MOUNTAIN HEIRESS
1481—SNOWED IN

**Rocky Mountain Safe House
*Safe House: Mesa Verde
‡Christmas at the Carlisles'
§§Special Delivery Babies

CAST OF CHARACTERS

Sarah Bentley—Owner of the historic Bentley's Bed & Breakfast. She's the maid of honor who's in charge of every detail.

Blake Randall—On the verge of retiring from the army rangers. The best man is well equipped to handle uninvited guests.

Emily Layton—The bride is Sarah's good friend.

Jeremy Hamilton—The groom works with Blake in the rangers.

General Charles Hamilton—Father of the groom. He works at the Pentagon and has a long list of enemies.

Ted Maddox—One of the general's aides.

Mike Alvardo—Another aide with high ambitions.

Senator Hank Layton—Father of the bride. He is a famously liberal politician from California.

Rebecca Layton—Mother of the bride.

Skip—His real name is Horatio Harrison Waverly-Smythe, and he's a speechwriter for the senator.

Honey Buxom—A belly dancer hired for the bachelor party.

Deputy David Kovak—In addition to law enforcement, he is involved in search and rescue and knows everyone in the area.

The Reuben twins—Young men who help out at the B and B.

Norman Franks—A mysterious figure who is an explosives expert.

Tyler Farley—The leader of a gang of local hell-raisers.

Chapter One

"Slow down, Sarah. The drop on this side of the trail is killer."

"It's only sixteen feet." Sarah Bentley paused to aim her flashlight beam over the edge where the light was swallowed by the dark of a cloudy, moonless night. With a shrug, she resumed walking, her boots crunching on the frozen snow. "I wouldn't even call this a cliff. It's a gradual drop-off. You've been on ski slopes that were steeper."

"Not in the middle of the night," her friend Emily Layton protested. "Not when I wasn't wearing skis."

This forest trail led from Bentley's Bed-and-Breakfast past the drilling site for Hackman Oil, and it followed a relatively straight line, which meant it was the shortest distance between the two points. But shorter didn't always mean faster. Sarah questioned the logic of taking this route. She halted on the path and turned to face her friend. "Why didn't we drive?"

"The text message from BOOM said to use the trail." Emily's breath formed a frosty little cloud around her wide, usually smiling mouth. "Specifically. The trail."

"I don't take orders from those jerks." She didn't like BOOM, a radical environmentalist group prone to one stupid thing after another. "What kind of mess am I walking into?"

"I already told you." Emily rolled her eyes and stamped her foot, acting more like a teenager than a twenty-eight-year-old woman who was about to be a bride. "I got a midnight text that said BOOM was going to send a message to Hackman Oil. They want me to join them and warned me to be quiet and take the forest trail. I needed you to show me the way."

Sarah pulled on the earflaps of her knit wool cap. She remembered being wakened and putting on her snow pants and parka over her flannel pajamas, but the reason for this middle-of-the-night hike through the frigid February night was still hazy. As a professional innkeeper who had been running the B and B for five years on her own, she should have developed a knack for snapping wide-awake at a moment's notice, but that talent had always eluded her.

Again, she wondered what she'd gotten herself into. Surely she hadn't agreed to join forces with BOOM. "What kind of message?"

"A protest. I'm guessing that it's something like spray painting graffiti on the sides of the trucks."

"I don't support the destruction of private property." Vandalism was never a good solution. Jerks like the leaders of BOOM, which stood for Back Off Our Mountains, caused more problems than they solved.

"I don't like it, either." Emily tucked a blond tendril under her cap. "In fact, I've decided to quit BOOM."

"That would make a lovely wedding present for your fiancé."

"Ha, ha, ha," she said. "You're so funny."

"I think I've heard him refer to BOOM. What did he call them?" Sarah couldn't resist teasing. "Eco-idiots?"

"That was after they dressed up like wolverines to bring attention to that endangered species. Not their finest hour."

"But very entertaining, especially the guy who got confused and dressed like Hugh Jackman in *X-Men.* Let me tell you, if Mr. Jackman was endangered, I'd get behind the protest."

"Most of the time, Jeremy and I have a strict agree-to-disagree policy. We don't discuss our causes."

In light of their vast differences of opinion, that was a wise policy. In four days, free-spirited Emily would be getting married at Bentley's B and B to her army ranger sweetheart, Jeremy Hamilton. Though their ideas might be volumes apart, Emily and Jeremy were on the same page when it came to their love. When they were together, they positively glowed. Sarah didn't understand their relationship. It could be one of those opposites-attract things. Or it could be kismet. Or Jeremy could be terrific in bed.

Whatever the case, she hoped their passion would be enough to see them through the larger problem: their families. Emily's father was a liberal senator from California, and Jeremy's dad was a four-star general. At the wedding, they would come face-to-face for the first time.

When Mr. Dove met Mr. Hawk, Sarah expected fireworks. She patted Emily's arm. "You have enough to worry about. Let's go back to bed."

"We're not turning back. We need to go to the drill site and talk sense into these guys."

"Why do you care?" She vaguely recalled a tidbit of gossip. "Didn't you used to date somebody from BOOM?"

"I'm thinking of you," Emily said emphatically. "You're going to get blamed for whatever damage they cause. Your B and B is only a mile and a half away from the drill site, and you've been fighting Hackman Oil for years."

"Legally fighting," she said, "through sanctioned environmental agencies and the courts and—"

"I know. But how will it look?"

"Good point." Damage at the drill site would look like she was lashing out and trying to get even. The Hackman Oil attorneys would be thrilled to have a reason to sue her, even if she was totally innocent. "We have to stop them."

"See? I'm right. I'm watching out for my girl."

Sarah shone her flashlight beam in the direction of the B and B. "At least, let's go back and get the truck. Sure, it's five miles of winding roads to access the site. But driving will still be faster...and warmer."

"It's better if we're quiet. I don't want Blake to know what I'm doing."

"Blake Randall?"

"Is there another Blake staying at the B and B?" Emily smirked. Apparently, it was her turn to tease. "Don't pretend that you didn't notice him. I saw your eyes melt like big, gooey chocolate drops when he walked through the door tonight."

"Of course I noticed." How could she overlook a man who was well over six feet tall and muscular enough to lift a Chevy truck with one hand?

"When you shook his hand, you blushed a darker shade of red than your hair."

"I'm not a redhead. It's strawberry-blond. And why shouldn't Blake know what we're doing?"

"He'd want to come with us."

Sarah didn't see a problem with that. "So?"

"I adore Blake," Emily said. "He's going to be the best man at our wedding. But he's an army ranger, and he has a temper. If he gets ticked off, he might go ballistic."

"An angry, hulking ranger might be exactly what we need."

Emily took a step forward. "Let's keep moving. I want to get this over with."

Sarah grumbled, "I'm too old for this."

"Oh, yeah, you're an ancient thirty-two."

It felt ancient. Sarah tromped forward. On her right was thick, dark forest. To the left were a few scraggly trees and rocks and the sixteen-foot drop-off. She knew every inch of the land surrounding her B and B and had labeled the nature trails with burnt wood signs so her guests could take hikes and not get lost. This path was called the High Road. If you followed it all the way to the end, beyond the site where Hackman Oil had started drilling, you reached a granite ledge with a panoramic view of the Elk Mountain range outside Aspen. Sadly, that spectacular sight would be blighted by noise pollution from the oil rig left behind after Hackman finished their work. The pristine forest would never look or feel the same.

Using the nonprofit business she ran, the Forest Preservation Society, she'd done everything she could to stop them. In other battles, she'd kept Hackman from drilling in four other locations but had lost this fight which was, ironically, the one closest to her doorstep.

From the path to her right, she saw bright lights shining through the trees, spooking the nocturnal wildlife. This intrusion was so wrong. Frustration and anger surged through her. Though her outrage was caused by the oil company, she could use this energy to argue with the jokers from BOOM.

She veered off the trail and paused at the edge of a wide clearing where she saw a flatbed truck with the Hackman Oil logo, a metal drill pipe stacked in the snow and the derrick hung with lights like a grotesque Christmas tree. A dark-colored van was parked near the entrance to the site. About twenty yards away were four men in parkas and work boots. One of them had a semiautomatic assault rifle slung over his shoulder. They all wore black ski masks.

"Why are they masked?" Emily asked in a whisper.

"There might be surveillance cameras." If so, Sarah's presence at the site would be on record as soon as she stepped into the light—an unfortunate fact that would please the Hackman attorneys. "I'm more worried about the assault rifle. They aren't planning to shoot up the equipment, are they?"

"Liam would never do anything like that."

"Is that the ex-boyfriend? Liam?"

"Yes."

Sarah shot her a glare. "Do I need to remind you that you're getting married in four days?"

"It's not like that. I've been friends with Liam for ten years, and I don't want to see him thrown in jail."

Sarah hoped to avoid a similar fate. She was about to drag Emily back to the B and B, but their whispering had attracted the attention of the masked men. The one with the semiautomatic pointed the barrel of his weapon in their direction and yelled, "Who's there?"

"Don't shoot." Sarah pushed the bare branches of shrubs aside and stepped into the light of the clearing. "I came here to talk."

"Hi, guys." Emily popped up beside her. "It's me, Emily."

"Emily Layton?"

"You sent me a text." She squinted in their direction. "Where's Liam?"

A man in a faded red parka stepped forward. "He couldn't make it, but don't worry. You can trust me."

As a general rule, Sarah never trusted anyone who said "trust me." When Emily started to stroll toward the masked men, she caught hold of her arm. "Stay close to me."

"Why?"

A lethal weapon was pointed in their direction;

Emily shouldn't need more explanation. "Do you recognize these guys?"

"Not with the masks."

Sarah called out, "What's your name?"

"You can call me Ty." He might have been smiling. It was hard to tell with the ski mask. "We didn't expect Emily to have company."

"I'm Sarah Bentley. I own the B and B and I've spent years fighting the oil companies."

He came halfway across the clearing toward them. "Nice to meet you, Sarah."

"Stop." She held up her palm. "I mean it. Not one more step."

"Fine." He halted.

"I'm not on your side," she said, "and I sure as hell didn't come here to participate in any sort of vandalism."

"Why are you here?"

"To warn you. There's nothing to be gained by damaging property. Believe me, I've done everything possible to stop the drilling, but Hackman followed all the correct procedures. We can't win this one. You should go home."

"You're not giving the orders."

"I'd be happy to give you an in-depth explanation of my position. First, tell your friend to put his gun down."

Ty glanced over his shoulder at the other three men, and then he looked back at her. "We're going to do this my way. If you cooperate, nobody gets hurt."

"Why would you want to hurt us?" Emily pulled her cell phone from her pocket and held the screen toward him. "Read the text. You invited us."

Ty held out his hand. "Let me see that text."

Dutifully, Emily walked toward him.

Sarah was more apprehensive. This felt like a trap. If Emily got too close to Ty, Sarah feared she would never see her friend again. Darting forward, she caught hold of Emily's wrist above her glove and tugged. "We're leaving."

Emily balked. "I'm just going to—"

"Now," Sarah said.

Ty came at them, moving fast. His arm shot out and he grabbed Emily's other arm. With a hard yank, he wrenched her away from Sarah's grasp, pulling so hard that Emily stumbled and fell to one knee. She let out a yelp.

Sarah didn't have the physical strength to fight with Ty, much less to take on all four men. Their only chance was to run. She drew back her arm and took a swing. Using her heavy-duty metal flashlight, she whacked Ty below the elbow. "Let her go."

"What the hell?"

Sarah hit him again. He could have fended her off, but Emily was struggling against him. As soon as he released her, Sarah and Emily dashed toward the trees at the edge of the clearing.

A blast of gunfire exploded in the still forest night. The sound rattled her, but she kept going, dragging Emily with her. Those were warning shots. A semiautomatic rifle wouldn't miss at this distance.

"Stop," Ty yelled. "I don't want to hurt you."

"Could have fooled me," she muttered as she and Emily charged through the trees and found the trail. "No flashlights."

"Right."

This section wasn't wide enough for them to go side by side. Sarah clutched Emily's arm and guided her, managing a clumsy trot. "Stay close. I know this trail."

From the clearing, she heard Ty crashing through the trees, yelling that he needed a flashlight. As soon as he had light, he'd locate the trail. When he did, he'd be able to run and catch up to them. They needed a different escape route.

Sarah dragged Emily to a full stop beside a granite boulder that bordered the steep side of the trail. She whispered, "We're going over the edge."

"Have you done this before?"

"Sure." That climb had been in the summer in full daylight when she could carefully pick her way. "We can do this."

"Show me how."

"Get down on your butt." She squatted beside the boulder. The cliff wasn't vertical, but the angle was steep. Below this ledge was a wider area that descended to a winding creek. "Follow me."

She dug her heels into the crusty snow, bracing herself so she could control her descent and not tumble head over heels. With her gloved hands, she grasped at rocks and clumps of frozen foliage. Emily followed.

Behind them, she heard more shouting and gunfire. The bursts from the semiautomatic were met with single shots. It sounded like a battle. She could only hope that whatever was happening at the clearing would provide enough of a distraction for her and Emily to get away.

Inching slowly and carefully, she was halfway down the hill when she heard a frantic gasp from Emily. "I'm slipping."

There was no place for Sarah to go. She steadied herself and prepared for impact as Emily collided with her backside. Sarah couldn't hold them both. Together, they careened the rest of the way down the incline and sprawled at the bottom.

"I'm sorry." Emily's voice was a whimper. "Are you okay?"

Sarah wiggled her arms and legs. No broken bones. Tomorrow, there would be bruises. "I'm fine."

Huddled together at the bottom of the slope,

they listened to shooting and yelling and a car engine starting. Emily stared up the hill. Even in the moonless night, Sarah could see the whites of her eyes and her fear.

"What's happening?" Emily whispered.

"It sounds like they're fighting somebody else. Maybe somebody from the oil company?" Sarah glanced at her. "We should call the sheriff. Do you have your cell phone?"

"I dropped it in the clearing."

"Follow me. Try not to make noise."

Though Sarah wanted to believe they were invisible at the foot of the cliff, she knew better. Anyone who knew about tracking would see the disturbance at the edge where they'd gone over. They needed to put more distance between themselves and the men in ski masks…or the men from the oil company. One was as bad as the other.

She picked her way through the forest. There were no marked paths in this area, but the trees thinned as they got closer to the creek. She paused to listen. "I don't hear shooting."

"Is that good?"

Either they'd left or they were spreading out in the forest to search. "I don't know."

Crouched beside a boulder, she looked back toward the ledge. In daylight, she would have had a clear view. She saw the beam of a flashlight and pointed. "They're coming."

Emily ducked down beside her. “What now?”

“Stay quiet.”

The flashlight beam bobbled along the path. When he passed the boulder where they made their desperate slide, her tension lessened. Maybe he wouldn’t notice their escape route. Maybe they’d be safe.

The beam scanned the forest. Though she knew the light wasn’t powerful enough to penetrate this darkness, she crouched lower, wishing she could disappear.

The light came back toward the granite boulder.

“Emily?” a deep, male voice called out. “Emily, are you out here? It’s Blake.”

Blake—the hulking, angry ranger—had come to their rescue. Sarah was so relieved that she almost burst into the “Hallelujah Chorus.”

Chapter Two

Blake Randall hadn't expected to start his duties as best man by rescuing the bride and her very attractive maid of honor, but tonight's action felt a lot more natural than getting decked out in his dress uniform and making a champagne toast. When he spotted the two women at the foot of the cliff, he anchored one hand to a tree at the edge of the path and threw down his belt for them to use as a climbing aid.

Emily grabbed his belt and scrambled up the steep slope and onto the path, where she threw her arms around him for a hug. In spite of the cold and the discomfort and a smear of mud on her cheek, she flashed a bright smile. "I'm so glad you're here. I was afraid something terrible would happen."

"Something terrible *did* happen," Sarah growled from the bottom. "Four masked men with guns tried to kill us."

"We don't know that for sure," Emily called

down to her. "I don't know why they were there or what—"

"Step aside," Blake interrupted her as he got into position to help Sarah. Though the threat had been handled for the moment, he couldn't be sure that they wouldn't be attacked again. It was imperative to get the women to safety as quickly as possible.

Sarah had removed her gloves to get a firm grip on his belt. As soon as she latched on, she climbed with sure steps. Her boots kicked through the crusty snow and found footholds. As soon as she was within his reach, he grasped her wrist to help her up the last few steps. Her arm slung around his neck. He felt her muscles tense. If they hadn't been dangling off the edge of a cliff, this hold might have counted as an embrace.

When she stood beside him on the path, she avoided his gaze. "Thanks, Blake."

"You could have made it on your own."

"Climbing uphill is easier than coming down." She straightened her shoulders. "We should get out of here."

"Agreed. My rental is in the clearing."

"Is it safe to go back there?" she asked. "How do we know they aren't waiting to ambush us?"

"We don't," he said, "but I doubt they've had time to regroup. I got in a couple of good hits before they drove off in their van."

"You shot them?" Emily squeaked.

Though he was certain that he'd wounded two of the men, he didn't intend to give her a recap. Emily was so bighearted that she'd want to seek out their enemies and offer aid.

Sarah was different. Her voice was calm as she said, "A couple of good hits, huh? Thanks, again."

"Let's go." He drew his Beretta and snapped a fresh clip into the magazine.

With the two women following, he moved quickly through the trees and back toward the clearing. Staying in the cover of the surrounding forest, they made their way toward the SUV he'd rented at the airport.

"Wait," Emily said.

"Keep moving," he said.

"We're going to be okay," she said. "Wait a minute."

His buddy Jeremy truly loved this woman. Blake found her unrelenting perkiness to be somewhat annoying. "What?"

"I see my cell phone over there. Can I get it?"

The bubblegum-pink phone struck an oddly feminine note amid the heavy-duty equipment and pipes. Leaving it behind would provide information to their enemies. He needed to secure the phone but didn't want to send Emily into an open area where she'd be an easy target if there was a sniper hiding in the trees. He handed his car keys to Sarah. "Get in the vehicle. I'll grab the phone and join you."

He watched as the two women climbed into the SUV. He hadn't expected Sarah to take the driver's seat, but that was what she did. Then she started the engine and drove toward him, providing additional cover. It was a smart move. He liked having her on his side.

In a few strides, he scooped up Emily's cell phone and dove into the passenger seat. The road leading away from the drill site was single lane for about a mile before it intersected with a regular two-lane road. If the guys in ski masks were planning to stop them, this would be a good place for an ambush. "I'll drive," he said.

"I've got it," Sarah said.

"There might be a need for evasive driving."

"Then you'd better fasten your seat belt."

She wheeled the SUV around and drove out of the clearing at top speed, which is exactly what he would have done. The headlights slashed through the dark as she expertly navigated the bends in the road. In seconds, they were approaching the intersection.

At the ninety-degree turn onto the more traveled road, the SUV fishtailed, but Sarah maintained control. On the two-lane road, her boot pressed down on the accelerator. With Sarah at the wheel, the boxy vehicle flew like a sports car, zooming through the trees.

Blake was impressed. "Where did you learn how to drive?"

"Mountains, high trails and frozen lakes," she said. The lights from the dashboard illuminated her grin. This was a woman who enjoyed going fast—his kind of woman. "I know my way around a skid."

"At the main road, go left."

"But the B and B is to the right," she said.

"I'm taking you ladies into town. We'll get a hotel room for the night and come back in the morning."

"I don't think so." Her grip on the steering wheel tightened. "I won't leave my property unprotected."

From the backseat, Emily piped up, "Is there anybody else staying at the B and B?"

"The last couple left this morning," Sarah said. "The whole place is reserved all week for the wedding party."

Belted into the passenger seat, there was nothing Blake could do when Sarah took a right turn and headed toward her bed-and-breakfast. This wasn't how things were supposed to go. He was accustomed to giving orders and having those orders obeyed. Keeping his voice calm, he reminded

Sarah of the danger. "They could already be there, waiting for us."

"You're right." She eased off the gas and pulled into a wide space on the road where the snow had been cleared. "We need to call the sheriff."

"I have it covered."

"What does that mean?"

Their situation had complications that went beyond the level of the Pitkin County sheriff's office. When he arrived in the area, he had contacted one of the local deputies, David Kovak, who was former military. "Drive into town. We'll get settled. And I'll take care of this."

"Are you saying that I should leave everything to you?"

He had the feeling that he was walking through a minefield. "I'm saying that I can help."

Keeping her hands possessively on the wheel, she turned toward him. Her dark eyes shone like obsidian. "I don't know you well enough to trust you. Not when my property is involved. Bentley's B and B has been in my family for over a hundred years, and I'm not going to be the Bentley who abandons it to vandals."

"Your survival is more important than your house."

"Why do you think this is so dangerous? How do you know?" Her voice was tinged with suspicion. "Come to think of it, how did you happen to turn up at the clearing in the nick of time?"

"I overheard Emily when she woke you."

"Did not," Emily said. "I listened outside your bedroom door, and it was totally quiet."

"I wasn't in the bedroom." He hadn't wanted to go into this explanation while they were parked at the edge of the road. Actually, he hadn't wanted to explain at all. That should have been Jeremy's job. But Jeremy wasn't here.

"What were you doing?" Sarah demanded.

"Checking out the B and B." He'd gone around the perimeter, tested windows and doors. Jeremy had told him that Bentley's was a secure location for the wedding, and Blake concurred. "With the addition of a few surveillance cameras, your B and B is practically a fortress."

"I'll take that as a compliment," she said. "Our guests have included international statesmen and presidents, starting with Teddy Roosevelt in 1907."

"Give me my phone," Emily said, leaning halfway into the front and holding out her hand. "I want to call Jeremy."

"Not yet," Sarah interrupted. "Not until we figure out what we're doing. How about it, Blake?"

He glanced between the two women. It would have been easier to face a dozen Taliban soldiers than to try to talk sense into Sarah and Emily. "I'll agree to go to the B and B. However, if there's any sign of disturbance or occupation, we'll get the hell out of there."

"Agreed," Sarah said as she slipped the SUV into gear.

In a few minutes, they were in sight of the heavy wooden stairs that led to the wide porch spanning the first floor. Two lantern-style lamps lit the porch, and another motion-sensitive light came on when they pulled into the parking area in front.

"Are these lights usually on?" he asked.

"Almost always," she said. "I know they were on when we left."

He didn't see any sign of disturbance but intended to use extreme caution. "You and Emily stay in the car. I'll need the key code for the front door."

"It's *F-E-R-R-E-T.*"

"Ferret?"

"The black-footed ferret is an endangered species."

Beretta in hand, he left the car.

SARAH KEPT THE engine running as she watched Blake approach her house. For such a big man, he was light on his feet, almost graceful as he went up the three stairs to the porch. With his cargo pants tucked into his black combat boots and the Beretta in his hand, he looked every inch a ranger, skilled in dealing with bad guys. She didn't doubt for a moment that he'd faced down four masked men. His cool competence under pressure was a little bit unnerving.

Emily climbed into the passenger seat next to her. "What are we supposed to do if somebody attacks Blake?"

"I hadn't thought of that." She could barely imagine Blake needing their help. But if she was wrong, if anything terrible happened to him, it was her fault. Sarah had insisted on coming back to the B and B instead of going to a safe hotel. "Open the glove compartment. Maybe he's got another weapon in here."

"Why?" Emily asked. "You're not thinking of going after him, are you?"

"I shouldn't have let him go in there alone." Her hand was on the door handle, ready to open it. "Did you find a gun?"

Emily pawed through the glove box. "There's nothing in here but rental documents."

Holding her breath, Sarah watched Blake punch the code into the pad by the front door. What if someone was waiting for him on the other side? What if he was met by a barrage of bullets? She couldn't just sit here like a helpless lump. She cracked the door to the SUV open. "I have to help."

"Sarah, stop. There's nothing you can do."

She glanced over at her lovely, delicate friend. Emily was a pale, blonde princess, the kind of woman who was destined to be rescued by a handsome prince on a white stallion. Not Sarah. She'd always taken care of herself and made her own way in the world. "Lock the doors and keep the engine running. If anybody comes after you, hit the car horn."

Before she could change her mind, she jumped from the SUV and rushed toward the house. At the same time, Blake opened the front door and charged inside. He must have hit the switches at the entryway because light splashed through the windows on the first floor. There was no sound of gunfire. No shouts. Nothing but the sound of her own footsteps as Sarah ran up the stairs and dove into the house.

Blake stood in the center of the large living room. His face was a mask of chiseled determination. His blue eyes narrowed, and he did *not* look happy to see her. "What are you doing here?"

"I thought you might need backup."

"Exactly how are you going to help?"

She went to the small supply closet behind the sign-in desk, opened the door and found a baseball bat—a security measure she kept in case of troublemakers and had never had occasion to use until now. "I'm armed."

"Okay, slugger, follow me and stay close. Turn on lights as we go."

Watching his back, she trailed him through the

dining room into the kitchen and the adjoining mudroom, where the outer door was safely locked. She took it upon herself to peek into the large pantry and the walk-in refrigeration unit, even though she couldn't imagine anyone hiding in there.

"Look for open or broken windows," he said. "There are only two other doors down here, correct?"

"One at the end of each hallway."

To the right, there were four bedroom suites, including her private area. Each had a king-size bed and private bathroom. Blake's vigilance was unflagging as he entered each separate room and searched with his Berretta held at the ready. His single-minded focus reminded her that this was more than a tour of her B and B.

She and Emily had been fired upon. They'd gone over the edge of the cliff to escape. Clearly, the guys in ski masks weren't with BOOM. Who were they? Why had they threatened her and Emily? They had to be after something. But what? She had the feeling that Blake knew more than he was saying, and she needed to get some answers from him.

When he bent down to examine the lock on a side door that opened onto a deck, she asked, "What are you looking for?"

"This door doesn't work on the keypad system."

"Only the front door," she said. "I lock the others

at night. There's a set of keys in my room and another set in the front desk."

"I'll need copies of those keys," he said.

Before she could ask why, he was striding down the hallway, and she had to run to catch up. At the other end of the B and B was a reading room with computer hookups that linked into a landline phone system. Wi-Fi was unreliable at the B and B, as were cell phones. Opposite the reading room was a game room. At the far end was the largest bedroom suite with an attached parlor.

After they'd checked the final door, she rested the baseball bat on her shoulder and asked, "Is it safe to bring Emily inside?"

He nodded. "It doesn't look like there's been a break-in. Just to be safe, I'll go upstairs. How many bedrooms are up on the second floor?"

"Eight," she said, "four single and four double. And the third floor is an open dormitory with twelve single beds. It's mostly used by scout troops and nature groups."

"What's your total capacity?"

"I've handled forty, but that's really too many." She didn't want to get sidetracked by a discussion of the B and B. "I have a couple of questions."

"Go ahead."

When he pulled off his cap, his dark brown hair fell over his forehead. Stubble outlined his chin, and she knew his look wasn't meant as a fashion statement; he just hadn't had time to shave. He was undeniably handsome but distant. His eyes were cool as glass.

As he gazed at her, Sarah realized she was still wearing her practical but unflattering wool knit cap with the earflaps. She must look like an idiot with her cap and her snow pants and her baseball bat. She yanked the cap off and made an attempt to fluff her hair. She unzipped her parka. Big mistake. Underneath, she was wearing flannel pajamas with puffy clouds and naked cherubs.

He raised an eyebrow. "Your questions."

"Right," she said. "Back at the clearing, how did you stop those guys?"

"They weren't expecting resistance, and I got the drop on them. I wounded two of them, shot one in the arm and the other in the leg." He shrugged as though that was nothing. "It's unfortunate they got away."

"Who were they? What did they want from us?"

He shook his head. "I'm not sure."

"If you had to take a guess, what would you—"

"Waste of time."

She tried a different tactic. "When I wanted to call the sheriff, you said it was covered. Did you talk to him before?"

"Thanks for the reminder." He took out his cell phone and punched in a number as he went down the hall toward the front door.

Sarah had no choice but to jog behind him. His big, tough ranger routine was wearing thin. She was tempted to tap him on the head with her Louisville Slugger. "Who are you calling?"

"I contacted Deputy David Kovak as soon as I arrived."

"He's a good man."

"You know him?"

"A little."

"Didn't think I'd need his assistance tonight, but I guess I was wrong."

While Blake had a terse conversation with the deputy and told him to come to the B and B, she planted herself on the staircase so he couldn't dash upstairs without talking to her first. As soon as he ended the call, she demanded, "You need to be honest with me. What's going on?"

"What time does Jeremy get in tomorrow?"

"Not until after noon. He's coming from D.C. with his father."

"And Emily's father?"

"The senator doesn't arrive until the day after tomorrow," she said.

Blake smirked. "When the two of them meet, all hell is going to break loose."

"Maybe it already has," she said. "Is what happened tonight related to the general or the senator?"

"Both men have enemies."

He came toward the staircase. Though she was standing on the second step, she was only a few inches taller than he was. His composure was truly disconcerting.

"What do you mean?" she asked. "What kind of enemies?"

His gaze met hers. For a moment, she caught a glimpse of concern in the depths of those very blue eyes. "The general has received death threats."

Chapter Three

Blake looked beyond Sarah's shoulder to the darkness at the top of the staircase. Since the doors to the outside remained locked and the windows intact, he doubted that he'd find any intruders hiding in the second-floor bedrooms. A greater potential for trouble came from the woman blocking his way. She didn't appear to be scared, but the pink blush on her cheeks betrayed a high level of emotion. She was angry. And he didn't blame her. Asking her to remain calm in the face of potential death threats was a lot. She loved this B and B and wouldn't want to see it turned into a battlefield.

"You should have told me." Her chin jutted out. "As soon as you arrived, you should have told me about the danger."

"I didn't know how serious it was." Not a valid excuse. "But you're right. You should have been informed."

"Who's making these threats?"

"We don't know." He glanced at his G-Shock

wristwatch. Kovak had promised to be here in half an hour. Blake had given him the license plate number on the van, and there might still be a chance to catch the four men in ski masks. "I should make a sweep of the upstairs before—"

"Whoa." She braced the baseball bat in front of her chest. "You're not going anywhere until you explain. Why is the general being threatened? Are we talking about terrorists?"

As a ranger, Blake had been trained in how to do an interrogation and how to withstand questioning. He could stonewall with the best of them, but those tactics didn't apply to a conversation with a pretty innkeeper. He and Sarah were on the same side.

"I'll be as truthful as I can," he said.

"That'd be a change of pace."

"What? I haven't lied."

"But you haven't told me everything."

"There wasn't much to tell. The threats haven't gone beyond the level of harassment. The general had his home office ransacked and his computer hacked. There was a bullet hole in one of his vehicles. He's been getting hate mail. It started when he was put in charge of a budget committee deciding which military bases and which hospitals will have their funding cut."

"A budget committee?" She sounded shocked. "These threats are about funding?"

"Everything in D.C. eventually comes around to money."

"It's so petty."

"But still dangerous. Homegrown assassins can be just as lethal as machete-wielding terrorists."

"But not those guys in the clearing," she said. "You didn't have much of a problem dealing with them."

Though he would have preferred coming off as a superhero who had handily defeated a team of highly trained hit men, her assessment was correct. "They weren't pros."

"Are you going after them?"

"When Kovak gets here, I'm going to try."

Standing on the staircase, she frowned as she tapped the head of the baseball bat against her palm. With her honey-colored hair curling in disarray and her parka open to show pink cherubs with round bottoms flying across her flannel pajamas, she should have looked ridiculous. But her erect posture gave her a certain dignity, and her dark eyes were serious.

"Go ahead and do what you need to do," she said.

"Are you giving the orders?"

"When it comes to my property, I am." Again, her sharp, little chin lifted in challenge. "You take care of the bad guys. I'll make sure that Emily and I are safe."

"How are you planning to do that?"

"Reinforcements," she said. "I'm going to call the Reuben twins to patrol the house and grounds. Both of these young men can shoot the fangs off a rattlesnake at a hundred yards."

"Are they reliable?"

"They've worked for me since they were fifteen. In addition to chopping wood and handyman repairs, they know how to make a bed and prepare a proper table setting."

He nodded his approval. "Make your call."

"Actually, the twins will be happy to meet you. Their family's hardware store hasn't been doing well, and the boys have been talking about enlisting."

Blake probably wasn't the best person to act as an army recruiter. At age thirty-five, he was on the verge of retirement and had just one last tour of duty in about six months. Though he'd dedicated his life to the military, he'd had enough of war. "Do you mind stepping aside so I can search upstairs?"

She leaned her back against the wall beside the staircase. "Knock yourself out."

As he climbed the stairs, he brushed past her and caught a whiff of a cinnamon scent, maybe her shampoo. A spicy fragrance suited her. In many ways, she reminded him of the strong, decisive women he served with.

The staircase bisected the upstairs hallway, and

the carved wood bannister extended to his left in a balcony that looked down over a two-story view of the entryway. This open area was probably meant as a staging place for guests hauling their suitcases upstairs, but it made a perfect spot for a spy to quietly hide and observe the comings and goings at the B and B.

Earlier tonight, when he'd taken his secret tour of the house, Blake had gotten a sense of protectiveness and security. The eight bedrooms on the second floor could be easily defended. They were inaccessible except by the central staircase and a narrow stairway at the south end that communicated with the kitchen and went down into the basement. As far as he could tell, all the windows had been upgraded to triple pane, a thickness that not only kept in the warmth but made the glass almost bulletproof. The doors were heavy and well fitted. Jeremy had been accurate when he compared this place to a modern-day fortress.

Blake checked the bedrooms one by one, looking in the closets, poking in the corners and peeking under the beds. The furniture was sturdy pine, polished to a high gleam. And the rest of the decor was simple—as clean as the West Point cadet barracks but not as spartan. In addition to a breakfast menu and a map of the local trails, every room had a hint of nature—simple things, like a basket of pinecones or a Christmas cactus or a rock garden.

He imagined Sarah planning these subtle touches that made her B and B feel welcoming and warm. He liked Bentley's Bed-and-Breakfast and hoped the wedding could be held here in spite of the attack in the clearing. This location was preferable to a hotel, where he wouldn't have as much control.

The third floor was a long, open room that extended all the way to the sloping eaves on one side. On the opposite side was a row of single beds against a pine wall that probably had storage behind it—a good hiding place with access through a padlocked door. Since the lock showed no sign of tampering, he felt satisfied that the area was secure.

Back on the second floor, he paused by the banister and looked down into the entryway where the two women were talking. Emily paced in an agitated dance. Her blond curls bounced in rhythm with her high-pitched voice as she waved her cell phone and ranted, "I can't believe Jeremy suggested that we have the wedding somewhere else. Or that we postpone. Getting everybody's schedule lined up was impossible." Her tone shot up to a screech. "Impossible."

Blake took a step back so he couldn't be seen. Confronting that blonde maelstrom was akin to a suicide mission.

"Calm down," Sarah said in her soothing alto. "Jeremy was just worried about you."

"This was exactly the wedding I wanted. And so did Jeremy. We never planned on a three-hundred-person fancy ceremony where we didn't know half the guests. Just family, just a nice cake and a few flowers on Valentine's Day, that's all I wanted."

"And that's what you'll have," Sarah promised. She'd changed out of her pajamas and parka to a pair of well-worn jeans and an oversize olive-green sweater with drooping sleeves that she'd pushed up on her slender wrists. She raked her fingers through her shining hair. Those vivid blond curls with the red highlights were the first thing Blake had noticed when they met. Then he'd been captivated by the intensity in her eyes with irises so dark that they were almost black.

"We should have eloped," Emily wailed. "Run off to Vegas and gotten married."

"You could still do that."

"I'm not going to take my vows in front of a fake Elvis." Emily stamped her little foot. "What does Blake say? It'd make a difference if he said we should do the ceremony here. Please talk to him, Sarah."

"Why would that make a difference?"

"Please."

Through the front windows, he saw the flashing lights of a police cruiser. Kovak had made good time in getting here. With any luck, he and the deputy could track down the men from the drilling site. Blake rushed down the staircase and opened the door. Two other officers accompanied Kovak. At a glance, Blake could tell that these were the kind of men he was accustomed to working with. They all wore Kevlar vests and police utility belts.

As soon as they entered, a truck pulled up and parked. Two husky young men bounded onto the porch—the Reuben twins. In their jeans, boots and parkas, they were a perfectly matched set with shaggy brown hair, stubble and toothy grins. Though the boys were doing their best to act cool, they quivered with excitement when they saw the bulletproof vests. Sarah pulled them aside to explain the situation.

Blake turned to Kovak. "Were you able to trace the license plate on the van?"

"The vehicle belongs to Tyler Farley." He spoke with a slow Western drawl. "Farley and his pals are known hell-raisers but I wouldn't have pegged them as assassins."

"Why not?"

"Too many beers. Too few brains."

As Blake had thought, Farley and his friends weren't pros. They hadn't even been clever enough to disguise their license plate. "Do they live nearby?"

"They've got a cabin about twenty minutes from here," Kovak said. "I already sent one of my men to keep an eye on the place. And I've alerted the local hospitals and emergency clinics. They'll call me if anybody shows up with a gunshot wound."

"Contact your man. See if he's close."

While Kovak made his call, Blake considered the possibilities. Farley must have been hired to pull off that stunt at the drill site. If they arrested him and his pals, Blake was sure he could convince these backwoods bad guys to give up the name of the person they were working for. The dangerous complication came from their possession of a semiautomatic assault rifle that probably had an illegal magazine capacity under Colorado's current gun laws.

Kovak held up his cell phone. "My man is there. The van is parked out front, and all the lights in the cabin are on."

"Tell him not to engage until we get there," Blake said. "If they leave, he should follow."

"Yes, sir," Kovak said. "I'm thinking we can bring these boys in without firing a single shot."

Blake was glad to hear they were on the same page. As soon as Kovak finished his call, he said, "Let's move. You take your car, and I'll follow."

A flash of strawberry-blond hair zoomed up beside him. "I'll ride with you."

Though she had a rifle in her hand, he wasn't about to let Sarah ride shotgun. "We had an agreement," he reminded her. "You stay safe, and I—"

"I promise not to get in the way." She looked toward Kovak. "Do you care if I tag along?"

"Always glad to have your help, Sarah."

Blake tried one more time to dissuade her. "You can't leave Emily here alone."

"I trust the twins to keep her safe. They're spending the night."

She dangled Blake's car keys from her fingers. "Should I drive?"

Without a word, Blake took the keys and headed for the door. He could think of only one reason Sarah would leave her beloved B and B to go after the bad guys: she wanted to talk to him about the wedding. Cake orders and flower arrangements were the last thing on his mind.

When he pulled away from the house, she fastened her seat belt and asked, "Have you talked to Jeremy yet?"

"Not yet."

"Good, because when you do I hope you'll tell him that the wedding plans shouldn't be changed. Emily has her heart set on this ceremony."

"My decision about where the wedding should be held will be based on risk assessment," he said coldly. "Protecting the general is my number one priority."

"But you're also the best man," she said. "That means it's your job to make sure the bride and groom are both happy."

"Don't tell me my job."

"For the bachelor party, are you planning to have a stripper? There's a tavern in Carbondale where they have a lot of stag parties, and you might want to check with them."

This was one relentlessly bossy female. He muttered, "I can find my own stripper."

"I bet you can. And I wonder what's your favorite type, the French maid or the naughty schoolgirl? Wait, I know. You're a dominatrix man."

"Are you volunteering?"

"I have my very own riding crop."

If she was trying to distract him, she'd succeeded. Though he kept his focus on Kovak's taillights, Blake's mind had wandered far away, visualizing long legs in fishnet stockings and a tight leather vest crisscrossing Sarah's breasts. His vision was an act of pure imagination. He hadn't seen enough of her body to know what she'd look like naked.

He yanked his thoughts back to the present situation. They were driving toward a potentially dangerous confrontation. He needed to have his wits about him. "Jumping in the car with me was a mistake, Sarah. A big mistake. I'd call it a third strike."

"What do you mean?"

"You disobeyed my order to drive into town. That was strike one. You followed me into the

B and B, that's two. Then you sashayed out the door and into that passenger seat."

"I never sashay," she said.

According to his imagined version of her, the sashay was only one of her moves. He cleared his throat. "I need your cooperation. When we get to Farley's cabin, you stay in the car. Got it?"

She nodded. "And when it's time to talk to Jeremy, what are you going to tell him?"

"I like your B and B as a location for the wedding. The house is secure and easily defensible. The location makes it difficult for anybody to sneak up on us. However, if there's a clear danger, we'll have to change plans."

"I really hope that doesn't happen."

On the road ahead of him, Kovak cut his lights and parked. Blake did the same. Before he left the car, he said, "Stay here, Sarah."

As she leaned across the seat and touched his arm, a glimmer of starlight touched her face. Her lips parted as though blowing a kiss. "Be careful."

She could look real sweet when she wanted to, but he wasn't fooled by her petal-soft lips and her long eyelashes. She was tough, determined and—like him—usually got her way.

He joined Kovak and his men. With a minimum of discussion, they had a plan. The officers would deploy around the front and rear of the one-story cabin while Blake went onto the porch beside the front door. Kovak would negotiate. Hopefully, Farley and his men would surrender without a fight.

Moving quickly, they got into position. Blake flattened his back against the wall between the front door and a window. He wanted to be close in case the guy with the assault rifle took it into his head to come out firing.

Kovak yelled, "Tyler Farley, this is Deputy David Kovak. We have your cabin surrounded. Farley, we know you're in there."

From the window to Blake's right, he heard a shout. "What do you want, Deputy?"

"Throw out your weapons. Raise your arms and come out one by one."

"Can't do that. One of my men can't walk."

"Drag him out," Kovak yelled.

Inside the cabin, they were arguing. Blake couldn't make out the words but knew from the tone that they disagreed. He suspected that the wounded men were ready to give up. The others might want to make a stand.

"Let's go," Kovak yelled. "You've got five seconds."

Blake silently cringed. If he'd been negotiating the surrender, he wouldn't have issued that ultimatum so quickly. Farley needed a minute to understand that it was to his benefit to cooperate.

"Hands up. Weapons down." Kovak started his countdown. "One…two…"

Beside Blake, the door swung inward. The guy who charged through and stood on the porch was still wearing his ski mask and held his assault rifle in one hand. He didn't notice Blake standing just behind him. Though the weapon was pointed down, his finger was on the trigger.

"Drop the weapon," Kovak yelled.

Red dots of light from the rifle sights of Kovak and another officer danced on the chest of the masked man. He didn't have a chance. Before he could lift his rifle, he'd be shot. The smart decision would be for him to surrender, but Blake guessed that this guy was operating more on impulse than intelligence.

In a well-practiced move, he knocked the masked man off his feet and onto his belly, face-down in the crusted snow. Blake took the rifle away from him and threw it aside. Straddling the other man's back, he aimed his handgun toward the house. "The rest of you, get out here."

Two others, unmasked, came onto the porch. One of them had a clumsy dressing on his upper arm. His face contorted in pain. "I need a doctor."

"Where's the fourth guy?"

"He can't walk."

Kovak and the other officers rushed forward. In seconds, they had taken Farley's ragtag crew into custody. While one of the sheriff's department's

SUVs drove the wounded men to receive treatment, Kovak and Blake questioned Farley.

Blake sat beside the handcuffed man in the back of Kovak's police cruiser. "Who hired you?"

"I don't know his name." Tyler Farley was a skinny guy with bad teeth. The permanent scowl etched into the lines of his thin face made it difficult to guess his age. "He told us it was a joke."

"How did he contact you?"

"On my cell phone." Spittle appeared in the corners of his downturned mouth. "He paid me three thousand bucks up front. Nobody was supposed to get hurt."

Blake didn't believe Farley was foolish enough to think their stunt at the drilling site was innocent. "What were you supposed to do?"

"Grab the girl. Emily Layton."

Kidnapping Emily could be leveraged into a threat against the general. "Then what?"

"When we had her, we'd make a call. The guy would tell us where to bring her, and he'd give us the rest of our money."

"Have you made that call?"

"Not yet."

Blake checked his wristwatch. Though a lot had happened, it had been less than two hours since he surprised Farley and his boys in the clearing. If he was going to get his hands on the person who hired Farley, he had to move fast.

Chapter Four

Sarah blamed her impulsive leap into Blake's SUV on an overdose of adrenaline racing through her veins. Her usual behavior was practical, and she didn't take unwarranted risks. But the successful escape from the clearing and the equally successful search of the B and B had blinded her to how violent the situation could become.

Sitting quietly in the passenger seat, she'd had a chance to calm down and regroup. While she'd watched Blake and the other men approach the cabin with military precision, she'd been tense. The yelling, the guns and the terrifying moment before Blake tackled that armed thug in the ski mask had turned her blood ice-cold. Even though the bad guys had been apprehended without a single shot being fired, the potential for danger was as obvious as a lit fuse that hadn't yet ignited the powder keg.

She owed Blake an apology. After seeing him in action, she understood why he didn't want her to interfere. He had a lot more to worry about than hiring a stripper for the bachelor party.

He yanked open the driver's-side door to his SUV and slid behind the steering wheel. Before she could apologize, he said, "I need your help."

"Me?" After the scene she'd just witnessed, she figured he could handle anything.

"Farley was hired by an unknown person to kidnap Emily. He's supposed to call his employer and arrange a meet. I'm going to make that call. If this guy wants to talk to Emily, can you play her part?"

"But I don't sound like her."

"I don't think he actually knows Emily. You can disguise your voice."

"Like this?" She changed her alto to a soprano and said, "Hi, I'm Emily and I'm getting married."

"Nice Minnie Mouse impression."

She tried again. "Hi, I'm Emily."

"Close enough." He started the engine for his rental vehicle and turned up the blower for the heater. "This background noise should disguise our voices."

"Why are you pretending to be Farley? He's sitting right over there in Kovak's car."

"I don't trust him to say the right thing. Are you ready to do this?"

Impersonating someone else was out of her comfort zone, but she wanted to help. "Okay."

As he punched in a phone number, he explained, "This is Farley's cell phone. I'm putting it on speaker."

A male voice answered on the fourth ring. "Do you have the package?"

"Hey, there," Blake said. "How'd you know it was me?"

"The caller ID, you idiot."

"I got the girl right here." Blake's smooth, deep voice had transformed into a thin drawl. "Where's my money?"

"You don't get paid until she's with me. You didn't hurt her, did you?"

"She don't like the handcuffs, but she's fine. Real fine and real pretty."

"Is she blindfolded? I told you to blindfold her."

"You bet she is," Blake said. "You want to talk to her?"

"Yes." The response was terse, almost a reprimand.

Blake held the phone toward her and said, "Go ahead, Emily."

Sarah tried to imagine how her friend would feel if she'd been captured. Emily wouldn't be crying; she was tougher than that. But she would be frightened. Putting a quiver in her throat, Sarah said, "Please, please, help me. If it's a ransom you want, my father will pay. He'll pay anything."

"Are you injured?"

"I'm scared," Sarah said. That wasn't a total lie. "You've got to help me."

Blake gave her a thumbs-up sign as he pulled the phone back. "Now you've heard her. Where do I bring her to get my payoff?"

"Come to the parking lot behind the Laughing Dog Saloon on the Bridge Road outside Carbondale. And make it quick. I expected to hear from you an hour ago."

"Well, ain't that too bad. Me and the guys had a little drink to celebrate."

"Don't bring your crew. Just you and the girl. Keep her blindfolded."

Blake disconnected the call, opened his car door and signaled to Kovak, who came toward them. Then he turned back toward Sarah. "Come with me."

"There's something I need to tell you first."

"What's that?"

In the overhead light from the car, she noticed his dark stubble, a smear of dirt across his forehead and the glittering intensity in his blue eyes. The sleeve of his parka was wet from his struggle with the armed man. "I'm sorry for getting in the way," she said. "I didn't take the threat seriously enough."

The corner of his mouth lifted in a half grin. "I appreciate that. You did a good job talking to that guy."

His compliment warmed her, and she had the irrational notion of doing whatever it took to please him. “I won’t cause any more trouble.”

Blake left the SUV to join Kovak, and Sarah followed. Standing in the forest between these two tall men, she felt as small as a mouse.

Blake filled Kovak in on the phone call and continued, “I was hoping Farley’s employer would give us a specific place, like a hotel room, where we could walk up to the door and arrest him. Instead, he’s treating this situation like a hostage exchange, probably because he doesn’t want to take a chance on Farley getting close enough to get a good look at him.”

“What about Emily?” Sarah said. “If he took her hostage, she’d be able to identify him.”

“Bad luck for her,” Kovak said.

“Maybe not,” Blake said. “He seemed concerned about her well-being and wanted her blindfolded. It’s hard to believe he intends to hurt her.”

“Kidnapping is a serious crime,” Kovak said. “Even if the kidnapper isn’t a pro, he won’t want to leave a witness.”

Sarah shuddered to think what might have happened if she and Emily hadn’t gotten away at the clearing. They hadn’t been prepared for danger. As trusting as Hansel and Gretel—or Gretel and Gretel—they’d followed a text message into the forest. Though she'd told Blake she was sorry, she couldn't help blaming him for not warning them.

"We need a plan," he said. "This might be our only chance to catch this guy."

"I can call for more backup," Kovak said.

"Not enough time. He expects Farley to show up soon." Blake gave a decisive nod. "And that's what we'll do. I'll take Farley's van and wear a ski mask. Kovak, you follow at a distance in my SUV. We'll keep in touch by phone. When I get close to the Laughing Dog, I'll put in another call to this guy. I'll distract him. You approach from behind. And we'll take him into custody."

"What about me?" Sarah asked.

"You've done enough," Blake said. "The other deputy is taking Farley to jail to book him. You can ride with him."

"Hold on," Kovak said. "What if our kidnapper wants to see Emily? Sarah could impersonate her."

"No way," Sarah said. "We don't look anything alike."

"She's right," Blake said. "They both have light-colored hair and are close to the same height, but that's where the resemblance ends. Emily is pale and dainty. Jeremy says she's like a perfect white rose."

And what did that make her? A big, old, prickly cactus?

Kovak squinted at her. "From a distance, Sarah

looks kind of like Emily, especially if she's got a blindfold covering half her face."

She muttered, "Or I could just put a bag over my head."

Blake ignored her and spoke directly to Kovak. "How well do you know Sarah?"

"Pretty well." He shrugged. "Why do you ask?"

"Most cops hate to have civilians involved, but you don't seem to have a problem with pulling Sarah along."

"We've worked together before." Kovak clapped her on the back. "Sarah regularly volunteers for mountain rescues. I've seen her in action, and she knows how to handle pressure."

"Thanks." She gave him a grin.

"To tell the truth, I'd rather have you setting the belaying lines for a descent than most of the guys in the sheriff's department."

"Good to know," Blake said as he headed toward Farley's van. "Sarah rides with me."

With Kovak's praise ringing in her ears, she strode along beside Blake. Maybe she wasn't a delicate flower like Emily, but she was the first woman the deputy would pick to play on his team. She'd always been "one of the guys." Not homecoming queen. Not the girl with tons of dates on Saturday nights. But men were comfortable around her and trusted her.

The interior of Farley's van was, predictably,

cluttered and grungy with a gross smell of stale bread, gunpowder and sweat. In addition to the litter—crumpled wrappers from fast-food places, empty ammo boxes and discarded clothes—there were filthy, blood-soaked rags, reminding her of the wounded men who had been arrested. She remembered her jolt of fear while watching the armed men and Blake circling the cabin.

She glanced over at him as he got behind the steering wheel. If she mentioned that she'd been scared, she knew he wouldn't want her to come along on this ride. With a shake of her head, she dismissed her nerves and concentrated on what needed to be done. "What should I use as a blindfold?"

"There must be something in here."

"Excuse me?" She wrinkled her nose. "I'm not touching anything in this van, much less putting it against my skin."

"See what you can figure using your clothes." He started the engine and pulled away from the cabin. "Do you know where the Laughing Dog is located?"

"Go left, then take a right at the main road." She unzipped her parka and looked down at what she was wearing. Her baggy sweater, jeans and underwear didn't provide much of a selection. "Instead of a blindfold, I could pull my cap down over my eyes."

"I don't expect to get close enough for this guy to make out details, but you heard him on the phone. He wants Emily blindfolded."

"Don't you have a scarf?"

"Don't you?"

There was an item of her clothing that might work. "I suppose I could use my bra. It's black."

"Is it lacy? Does it have those cups that poke out?"

"It's a sports bra." She couldn't believe she was discussing her underwear with him. "A cotton and spandex blend."

"Let me take a look at it."

Glaring at him, she took off her parka and pulled both arms inside her sweater. She wriggled the strap off one arm, pulled the bra over her head and took off the other strap. Though she hadn't exposed an inch of flesh, she felt exposed, and she was glad the lights from the dashboard weren't bright enough to reveal the heat she felt rising in her cheeks. At least she wasn't scared anymore.

Plunging her arms back into the sweater sleeves, she dangled the bra in front of him. "Ta-da."

"The perfect blindfold."

"Easy for you to say. You're not going to have a bra wrapped around your face."

"It won't be for long," he promised. "This maneuver needs to happen fast before the guy figures out what we're doing. It goes without saying that you'll stay in the van."

"I understand." She slipped back into her parka. "I have a question for you. If this person is trying to threaten the general, why kidnap Emily?"

"The general himself isn't a realistic target. He's a tough old bird, and he's usually protected by his aides. If the kidnapper had Emily, he could use her as leverage."

"To do what?"

"Could be something as simple as ransom," he said. "Or it could involve having the general change his position on some kind of finance bill. Attacking the family makes for an effective scare tactic. When it comes to his own personal safety, the general is fearless. But his family? He'd do anything—including going against his core principles—to protect them."

It sounded to her like he'd had some experience with this sort of operation. "Have you done things like this before?"

"I did some counterintelligence work in the Middle East, enough to know that terrorists don't always use explosives to get what they want. Fear is a powerful motivator."

Though she'd never been to war, she had an idea of what he meant. "You can't give in to fear."

"Can't ignore it, either," he said as he clipped a

hands-free phone into his ear. "I'm going to check in with Kovak."

Leaning back in the seat, she stared through the windshield at the cold, snow-encrusted forest on either side of the road. The mountains were a wonderful place to live. Nowhere else would ever feel like home to her. But she was well aware of the dangers hidden in these rocky slopes. Every winter, there were deaths due to natural causes.

Living here, you learned to be careful. But you couldn't let fear keep you locked inside in front of the fireplace. Without risk, life was too dull.

He ended his call. "The cell phone reception is better here than at your B and B. Earlier tonight, I tried to call Jeremy and the call got dropped twice."

"Is Jeremy with his father?" she asked.

"They're together, driving each other crazy."

"The general can't be happy about having his son marry into Emily's family. Her dad is super-liberal."

The corner of Blake's mouth twitched into a grin. "When those two shake hands for the first time, it's going to turn into an arm wrestling match."

"You think that's funny?"

"Hell, yes," he said. "Don't you?"

Because Emily was a good friend, Sarah had been sympathetic about her family problem. But she had to admit that she'd been looking forward to the confrontation. "I've been trying to think of conversation topics they might be able to talk about without arguing, like the weather or sports."

"Sports are out. The senator supports West Coast teams and the general likes the Yankees and Patriots."

She envisioned many long, uncomfortable silences with the two men snarling at each other. "Do you have any ideas? I'd guess that you and I don't have much in common. What would we talk about?"

"Mountain rescue," he said. "How did you get started with that?"

"I took a search and rescue course a long time ago. And I was already into rock climbing."

"Me, too."

It seemed that they actually did share some interests. "Do you ski?"

"Skiing and snowboarding, but I like cross-country best."

As did she. She'd learned cross-country skiing as soon as she could walk. "What about rodeo?"

"Not a big fan," he said. "My family used to have a farm in Wisconsin, so I got enough of horses and cows when I was growing up."

With that kind of background, she knew that he was familiar with livestock. "I've always been concerned about animal cruelty at rodeos," she said. “I cheer for the bucking bronco instead of the cowboy.”

“Cowboys aren’t your thing?”

“Not really.”

The light from the dashboard outlined his high cheekbones and sharp jawline. When he grinned again, she noticed that his lower lip was fuller than the upper. “You know, Sarah, I don’t think we’d have a problem finding things to talk about.”

When she first started talking, she hadn’t been on a fishing trip, trying to find out more about him. But that was what had happened. She’d learned that they had similar interests and small-town backgrounds. In that way, they were compatible.

And in other ways, too. Emily noticed Sarah’s first reaction when she met Blake. A glowing blush that spread from her neck to her hairline. Sarah had always preferred big men with broad chests and long legs. Seeing Blake in action was, well, it was kind of thrilling.

She ripped her gaze away from his profile and squinted down at her lap, pretending interest in the bra she held in her hands. She didn’t want to be attracted to him. This weekend was going to be difficult enough.

“Take a left up here.” They were making good time. No other vehicles on the road. And the pavement was dry. “We’re about ten minutes away.”

"Put on your blindfold."

Grumbling, she took off her cap and tied her bra around her forehead. When she flipped the front down, the black fabric covered her eyes, but she could still see through. She eased it up on her forehead. "This had better be worth it."

"If we catch this guy, we'll be on our way to ending the threat, and the wedding can go forward." He took Farley's cell phone from his pocket and held it toward her. "I should make contact with our mystery man. Press the redial button and hold the phone while I talk?"

She did as he asked and listened as the kidnapper answered on the first ring.

Using his fake drawl, Blake said, "I'm getting close. Where should we meet?"

"Changed my mind," the kidnapper said. "This project is over."

"What's your problem?" Blake shot her a worried glance. "I did what you wanted."

"Changed my mind," he repeated, angrily. "Never contact me again."

"You can't just cut me off like that. You owe me." Blake put a convincing whine into his voice. "What am I supposed to do with the girl?"

"Get rid of her."

A shudder ran through her. This man had called for Emily's death as casually as he'd order a pizza.

Playing along, Blake drawled, "Are you telling me to kill her? 'Cause that's going to cost you extra."

"Do whatever you want with her. Do it slowly, painfully. You boys can have yourselves some fun making her squeal. That will be payment enough for your services."

A muscle in Blake's jaw twitched but he kept his voice flat and emotionless. "You promised cash. Half up front and half now."

"Let's cut the crap. I know who you are."

"Is that so?"

The kidnapper's voice turned cold. "Don't play games with me. You're out of your league."

Abandoning his fake voice, Blake said, "We should talk."

"Oh, we will. Not today but soon. Good night, Major Randall."

The phone went dead.

Chapter Five

With a yank of the steering wheel, Blake pulled Farley's van off to the side of the road and parked. He took the cell phone from Sarah and hit Redial. The kidnapper's phone rang unanswered, a tinny echo in the night.

"What went wrong?" Sarah asked.

"He must have gotten wind of what really happened to Farley and his men." Not a big surprise. The men hadn't been operating under a cloak of secrecy. Someone might have contacted the kidnapper from the hospital. The kidnapper might be working with another person. Blake had known that arresting the kidnapper was a long shot. His hope had been that if they quickly executed their plan, they'd catch the guy off guard.

"He knew your name."

He shrugged. "It wouldn't be hard for him to identify me. He knows what's going on with the general, and I'm Jeremy's best man. Plus, I have reservations at your B and B."

"Oh, my God. That's terrible." She sounded truly alarmed. "If he got your name from my records, it means somebody who works for me was in contact with him."

"Not necessarily."

Her dark eyes flicked from side to side as she searched his face for an answer. "Give me another explanation."

"Are your records computerized?"

"Of course."

"He could have hacked the system."

"Even worse." She threw her hands in the air. "I keep everything on the computer. He could know every detail about the wedding. The timing, the suppliers, the arrival times for the guests…"

"There's another possibility." He needed to divert her attention before she worked herself into a wild frenzy. "He could have monitored our cell phone calls. Kovak could have said my name."

She dismissed that theory with a shake of her head. Though tied down by the black bra wrapped around her forehead, her hair bounced. "Damn it, Blake. You should have told me about the danger. I wouldn't have put all that info on the computer, where some psycho could hack into it. What did he mean when he said that creepy stuff about killing her slowly?"

"Trying to shock us."

"It worked."

Her nose wrinkled as though she smelled rotten eggs, and he was momentarily distracted by her expression. Even at two in the morning, after all they'd been through, she was bursting with energy. He wanted to tell her that everything was going to be all right. But he wasn't going to lie. They had plenty to worry about.

Deliberately looking away from her, he said, "I need to talk to Kovak."

He made the connection on his hands-free phone. After quickly filling the deputy in on what had happened, Blake launched a new plan for investigating. To Kovak, he said, "Since we're close to the Laughing Dog, we might as well start there. Meet us in the parking lot outside the saloon."

His hand rested on the gear shift knob. Sarah reached toward him. "Wait," she said. "There's something I need from you."

"I'm listening."

"From now on, I want to know everything. You've got to keep me in the loop. Will you do that?"

He wasn't accustomed to sharing intelligence with civilians, but he understood where she was coming from. The B and B was her responsibility, and she needed to take care of the place and the people who stayed there. "You have my word."

"Good." She gave a tight nod. "Keep going on this road. We're close to the Laughing Dog. I don't know what you hope to find there. It's been closed for hours, and it's Tuesday night so there wasn't live entertainment."

"Entertainment, huh?" He slipped the van into gear. "Is the Laughing Dog the place where you thought I should hire a stripper?"

"Get your mind out of the gutter. I'm talking about live music—country western bands or folk singers." She reached across the console to give him a shove. "Still, I guess it's a good sign that you're still thinking of strippers."

"How so?"

"If you need a stripper, you're still considering my B and B for the wedding location."

He couldn't promise a decision. "That's not my call."

The Laughing Dog Saloon stood alone on a separate block at the edge of the town. The two-story rough-wood saloon with a wide porch across the front reminded him of an old fort. In the back, the spacious asphalt parking lot was cleared of snow. A light above the back door shone down on two trucks and another late-model vehicle.

"The owners live upstairs," she said. "A really nice couple, but if you're planning to wake them up, you might want to wait until Kovak joins us."

He parked Farley's van beside one of the trucks and looked over at her. "And you might want to take off your bra."

She snatched the black fabric off her head and ran her fingers through her shimmering reddish-blond hair. Those curls were the only soft thing about her. In spite of the occasional flashes of cuteness, her features were strong, set in a triangle-shaped face with a sharp, determined chin.

This night had been stressful, and she'd handled it well. He wanted her to know that he appreciated her courage. Reaching toward her, he tucked a strand of hair behind her ear. "You're a good sport."

She grabbed his hand and pushed it away. "Yeah, that's me. Good, old Sarah."

He wasn't sure why she sounded ticked off. "You don't have to bite my head off."

"Just keep your hands to yourself." She sank down in the seat, pulling her head into her parka like a turtle going into its shell. "I don't like being teased. When I was a kid and guys pulled my pigtails, I never thought it was funny."

"I bet you got back at them on the playground."

She cast a baleful glance in his direction. "None of those jerks ever teased me twice."

"You think you're pretty tough."

"That's right."

Her attitude sounded like a challenge, and he couldn't pass up a schoolboy urge to play games with her. He unfastened his seat belt and turned sideways to face her. "You'd probably hate it if I did this." With a lightning-quick move, he tugged down the zipper on her parka.

She unfastened her seat belt and whipped around in her seat to face him. The look in her dark eyes was half fury and half surprise. "I can't believe you did that."

"Because nobody messes with Sarah, am I right?"

"Nobody survives to tell the tale."

"Let me fix this." He reached for her zipper as though he intended to pull it back up. As soon as she glanced down, he lightly tweaked her nose.

With zero hesitation, she bolted from her seat and crossed the space separating them. Her right arm cocked, and she took a swing at him. Blake was faster. He caught her wrist before her fist struck his chin.

As she yanked to get away, she came closer to him. A different sort of urge raced through him. He wanted to kiss the snarl off those full lips, to feel her body pressing against him. But that was definitely inappropriate. He could barely justify the teasing. Forcing her to kiss him was out of the question.

He released her hand and faced forward, staring through the windshield. "You know, those boys who pulled your pigtails only wanted you to notice them."

"Is that what you want?"

A breathless quality in her voice caught his attention, and he turned toward her. “Maybe.”

Her left hand stroked his cheek. She maneuvered closer. Her gaze fastened to his mouth. Inches away from him, her right hand climbed his chest to his throat then his jaw. Gently, she caressed his cheek. Her eyes sent a message as though she wanted to kiss him. Instead, she pinched his nose between her thumb and forefinger and squeezed twice. “Honk, honk.”

Before he could react, she was out of the van. Pacing around to the front, she laughed and said, “Never tease me twice.”

When he joined her, a light went on in the upper half of the saloon building. A bearded man in red flannel underwear stepped onto the landing for the outdoor staircase. He was holding a rifle.

“We’re closed,” he yelled.

“Hey, Zeke.” She waved to him. “It’s Sarah Bentley.”

“What are you doing here? Is that Farley’s van?”

Kovak pulled into the lot behind them and parked the rental SUV. He also waved and identified himself. “We need to ask you a couple of questions, Zeke.”

“Meet me at the back door.” Zeke disappeared into the upper part of the house.

In spite of the late hour, Deputy Kovak was alert and ready to jump into an investigation with both feet. "I'll start by tracing the kidnapper's phone number," he said. "It's probably a burner phone with no identification, but I'll try. As soon as I get back to the jail, I'll question Farley. Do you want to be with me for that, Blake?"

"Not necessary."

"Do you think the kidnapper is a local? Or somebody who lives in Aspen?"

"I don't know," Blake said. He was still distracted by Sarah honking his nose and thinking about how he could get back at her and get closer to her at the same time.

"Here's what I'm thinking," Kovak said. "A local would know that Farley was a bad guy who could be hired to help with a kidnapping."

"But the plot against the general doesn't have roots in this area."

The back door opened, framing Zeke in his faded long underwear. His full salt-and-pepper beard compensated for thinning hair above his heavily lined forehead. The man was huge. When he gestured for them to enter, he looked like a grizzly bear swatting at a horse fly.

Through the back door, they passed through a clean, modern kitchen that had been washed down for the night. The front area of the saloon was a large, wood-paneled room with a long, oak bar on one side and a stage on the other.

Zeke pointed to a round table. "Have a seat. You want coffee?"

Sarah answered for them. "Coffee is too much trouble. How about tea?"

"I hate tea," Zeke muttered.

"Coffee it is," she said. "I'll make it."

As she went into the kitchen, Blake introduced himself and sat at the table. "Tyler Farley and his friends are in trouble. Two of them are in the hospital."

"How were they hurt?"

"Gunshot wounds."

Without moving, Zeke bellowed, "Dolly, get your tail down here. You'll want to hear this firsthand."

Dolly must have already decided the same thing because she popped through a door at the edge of the stage and bustled toward them. She was an imposing figure, not especially tall but big. Her frizzy blond hair made a halo around her head. She adjusted her long, flannel robe as she sat. "Who got shot?"

After Kovak introduced her as Zeke's wife, he gave the names of the two men. "They're under arrest at the hospital and ought to be okay."

"What happened?"

In an area like this where everybody knew everybody else's business, Blake figured it was hopeless to keep secrets. The arrest of Farley and his gang would be gossip fodder for days. He kept his explanation simple. "Farley was hired to kidnap Emily Layton, who is staying at Bentley's B and B."

"And getting hitched this weekend," Dolly said. "Go on."

"We stopped them." Blake avoided details of his own exploits. He didn't need to build up his rep as a tough ranger. On the other hand, he didn't want to be known as the guy who Sarah honked. He cleared his throat. "Deputy Kovak and his men arrested four men at Farley's cabin. The kidnapper who hired them arranged to meet here at the Laughing Dog, which makes me think he's been here before."

Sarah emerged from the kitchen carrying a tray full of mugs and a coffeepot, which she set on the table. "Help yourselves."

Dolly gave her a grin. "Hi, sweetie. Are you all set for that fancy wedding?"

"It's not that fancy. Just family." She gave Blake a fake, innocent smile. "This is the best man."

"I'll bet he is," Dolly said.

After he poured his coffee, Kovak asked, "Have you seen Farley in the past couple of days?"

Dolly answered. "He was in here last weekend. We had Jessie and the Outlaws playing, and the joint was packed. Farley got into a brawl, and Zeke had to drag his skinny tail outside and have a chat."

"He settled down pretty quick," Zeke muttered. "I let him come back in."

"Why?" Kovak asked. "If he was being a troublemaker, why not send him on his way?"

"He was flashing a big, old wad of cash and buying drinks for his pals."

Already spending the cash he'd been paid by the kidnapper. Blake wasn't surprised. Farley hadn't struck him as particularly intelligent or sophisticated.

"Over the past week," Kovak said, "have you noticed any out-of-towners?"

"Well, sure, on the weekend. When we've got a good band playing, we get a crowd," Dolly said. "Nobody stood out."

"Anybody who was dressed weird," Blake suggested, "maybe wearing a suit. Or sitting alone."

Both Zeke and Dolly shook their heads. Zeke paused. His brow furrowed as he concentrated. "I noticed something the other day. It must have been Sunday because I was dead beat, sitting out in the back, enjoying the sunny weather and thinking about how I was sick and tired of winter. There was a shiny, new SUV parked by itself in the back of the lot. And the driver was behind the steering wheel. I figured he was making a phone call."

"What color was the vehicle?" Blake asked as he took a sip of coffee.

"Black or dark blue. I'm not sure which."

"The make?"

"Maybe an Escalade," Zeke said. "I had the feeling that it was a rental."

When he started to pour himself a mug of coffee, Dolly slapped his hand. "None for you, Zeke. You'll never get back to sleep."

He grumbled but tucked his hand into his lap.

"If he's not a local," Kovak said, "I can check with the car rental places in the area. And I can get registries for the hotels. Blake, do you have any idea about his name?"

"If I scan those lists, I might see someone familiar."

Dolly turned her focus on him. "Tell me about yourself, young man. Are you single?"

He nodded. "Yes, ma'am."

"Did you hear that, Sarah?" Dolly beamed at her. "He's not married."

"I'll be sure to alert the media," Sarah said drily.

"No need to be cranky." Dolly's smile got even wider. "And I'll bet you're in the military like Emily's beau."

"Army ranger," Sarah said.

"Not for much longer." He didn't owe anyone an explanation, but he found himself looking at Sarah as he explained. "After I'm done my last tour of duty in about six months, I'm set to retire."

"It's time for you to make a change in your life," Dolly said with assurance. "I've been tending bar for twenty-three years, and I can read human nature."

"Is that so?"

"You have the look of a man who's ready to settle down, maybe find yourself a wife and have a couple of kids."

He didn't say no.

Chapter Six

One of the things Sarah liked best about running a bed-and-breakfast was that she didn't usually have to prepare other meals. Muffins, waffles, omelets and oatmeal usually filled the bill. During the rest of the day, she provided snacks and drinks and sandwiches, but she wasn't actually expected to tie on an apron and cook.

But here she was, standing in the walk-in pantry at ten o'clock in the morning, thinking about what she should make for lunch. A wide variety of canned goods stood at attention on the shelves, with the lima beans shoulder to shoulder beside the creamed corn and the chicken broth. Kind of a hodgepodge. A real chef would have been more organized. Again, why was she concerned about making lunch?

She could offer a repeat of breakfast. She'd already handled one small sitting when she'd thrown together an eight o'clock meal of bacon and eggs for the Reuben twins, who had stayed the night to stand guard. They'd had a bunch of wide-eyed questions about the shoot-out at Farley's cabin, and she'd been happy to report that not a single shot was fired. Her high-minded lecture had fallen apart when she'd admitted that Blake had wounded two of the men when he single-handedly took on all four in the clearing with the oil rig.

She reached for a can of crushed tomatoes, thinking she could get a sauce started now and have spaghetti with garlic bread. Why go to all that trouble? The only people she expected for lunch were Blake and Emily, which meant she could get by with a minimum of fuss. But for some reason she wanted to create a delectable, homemade, mouthwatering meal. Why? Who was she trying to impress?

Blake.

"Really," she muttered. Did she really need to prove to him that she was domestic? With a self-derisive snort, she shoved the tomatoes back onto the shelf.

Last night when Dolly had said that Blake looked like a man who was ready to settle down, Sarah had caught a glimpse of acknowledgment in his eyes. True enough, he was setting a new course for his life, retiring from active military duty.

But change didn't necessarily mean he was planning to find a wife and start popping out rug rats. Even if he was, his life decisions didn't have anything to do with her. Sarah wasn't applying for the job of wife. Running a B and B was all the responsibility she wanted or needed.

From the kitchen, she heard Emily groan. "Oh, my God. I need coffee."

Sarah poked her head out of the pantry. "I'll make some more."

Since she liked her coffee fresh, she made several pots a day rather than leaving a gallon of coffee sitting in the urn on the counter. Last winter, she'd purchased a cheapo espresso machine that never worked properly, and she was considering an upgrade to a more efficient model.

With another prolonged groan, Emily sank onto a stool at the center island. She dragged her fingers through her hair, which, although uncombed, fell in adorable curls framing her face. "I couldn't sleep. Jeremy and I were talking on the phone all night."

"Arguing?"

"Discussing."

That must have been some intense discussion. Emily was still awake when she and Blake returned at three in the morning. As Sarah rinsed the glass coffee carafe in the sink, she asked, "What's the decision? Does the wedding go forward as planned?"

"Yes," Emily said with uncharacteristic firmness.

"Yay."

"Jeremy isn't happy about it," she said, "but Blake changed his mind. And I have you to thank for that."

"Me?" Sarah measured whole coffee beans into the grinder. "Why thank me?"

"Whatever you said to Blake must have made an impression. I heard his half of the conversation with Jeremy, and Blake told him that you and I had gone to a lot of trouble planning the wedding. He said that the B and B is perfect for security, and we should go ahead and have the most romantic weekend of our lives."

The coffee grinder made a loud growl as Sarah tried to recall what she'd said. "I don't remember mentioning romance."

"That might have come from me," Emily admitted. "I love the mountains. Jeremy and I met on the ski slopes. We shared our first kiss three years ago on New Year's Eve at the Hotel Jerome in Aspen. The light, drifting snow was the most beautiful sight I've ever seen."

"You're the romantic, all right." Sarah finished preparing the coffee and came around the island to stand behind her friend. She rubbed Emily's shoulders. "You could reach into a bushel of onions and pull out a sweet-smelling rose."

"Last night, all my romantic promises didn't do a bit of good with my reluctant groom," she said. "It took Blake about five minutes to make

Jeremy change his mind. He's a good guy, don't you think?"

"Does it matter what I think of Blake?"

"It could." Emily spun around on the stool and looked her in the eye. "Blake told Jeremy that he envied us. He said that he was ready for marriage and looking for an Emily of his own."

"That lets me out," Sarah said.

Though she and Emily had been friends for years, they were very different women. Emily cooperated. Sarah took charge. Emily was an optimist. Not so much with Sarah. When she looked at a garden, she saw the weeds and knew they had to be pulled. Emily reminded her of a distant cousin she'd just met, Gabriella, who was on her way to getting married to one of the hottest cowboys in Pitkin County.

Women like Emily and Gabriella were the ones who collected marriage proposals, and that was a fact. Rough, tough men like Blake wanted soft, sweet ladies when it came to settling down. He'd prefer Sarah for a friend, of course. Not for a mate.

"What time are Jeremy and his father arriving?"

"They'll get to the airport in Aspen at about two and rent a car. They should be here by three. And the general will have two of his aides with him."

Sarah heard a hint of tension in Emily's usually melodic voice. In spite of her optimism, she was worried. "Do you call Jeremy's dad the general?"

"To tell you the truth, I try to avoid calling him anything." She rolled her eyes. "His first name is Charles, but he's not a Chuck and definitely not a Charlie. And I can't imagine calling him Dad."

"Is he going to be wearing his uniform and medals?"

"I seriously hope not."

Sarah went to the counter and lifted the lid on an old-fashioned bread box. Inside were a couple of blueberry muffins from yesterday and a loaf of homemade wheat bread. "Would you like toast with your coffee?"

"I would," Blake said as he stalked into the kitchen. He was dressed in a parka and jeans. His face was ruddy as though he'd been outside in the cold. "Scratch that. I'm hungrier than toast. Did I see ham in the fridge?"

"How long have you been awake?"

"I got up a little after you," he said.

She'd been out of bed at seven-thirty. "Why haven't I seen you?"

"I went right to work." He unzipped his parka. "I wanted to get my surveillance cameras placed. And the terminal for my satellite phone hooked up."

"I hope you realize that during a heavy snowstorm none of those fancy wireless devices are going to work."

"I'm aware," he said. "My next project is to interface with your landline and computer."

She looked down at his boots, glad to see they were clean and he hadn't tracked dirt through the house. "I have a couple of housekeeping rules."

"Shoot."

"If there's mud on the boots, they'd better be wiped clean or taken off at the door. There are hooks by the front door for your hat and jacket. And back here—" she pointed to the half glass kitchen door that connected to the mudroom "—you'll find more places to hang outerwear. I don't want to spend my whole day picking up after my guests."

When he snapped a crisp salute, she cringed. *Way to charm him, Sarah! Give the man a lecture about dirty boots.*

As he dropped off his jacket in the mudroom, she placed the loaf of bread on the cutting board and took out a knife.

"I'd rather have a muffin," Emily said. "Blueberry?"

"Right."

Sarah put together a plate for Emily with a muffin and a smear of cream cheese. But her focus stayed on Blake as he emerged from the mudroom. Under the parka, he'd been wearing a black turtleneck that outlined the breadth of his chest and his lean torso. His jeans looked new, and she wondered if he'd bought them especially to come to the mountains.

Lifting her gaze to his face, she noticed that he still hadn't shaved. The stubble on his chin was turning into a beard. The dark brown hair falling over his forehead made his eyes seem even bluer. Aware that she was staring, she looked down at the cutting board. "Did you want a sandwich now? Or would you rather wait for lunch?"

"Were you planning something special for lunch?"

Was she? "I don't know."

"Don't bother," Emily said. "There's going to be a mob for dinner with Jeremy and his dad and the two aides. I'll help you put something together."

"I can do my own sandwich," he said as he came toward her and took the bread from her hand. "Out of the way, Sarah. Honk, honk."

She glanced up sharply. He was grinning, and she matched his smirk with one of her own. Last night, she'd honked his nose. That was the kind of relationship they had. Forget the mesmerizing blue eyes and the sexy body—they were pals.

Taking the bread from him, she said, "I'll do the sandwich. I'm the hospitality professional here."

"Is it okay if I pour my own coffee?"

"Help yourself."

"Here's another rule," Emily said. "Feel free to help yourself to food during the day, but always put your used dishes in the sink. And never ever start the dishwasher."

"You've been here before," he said to her.

"I worked here for a summer," Emily said. "That's how Sarah and I got to be friends. Ski season was over so I was done with teaching the snow bunnies, but I didn't want to leave the mountains."

"Didn't want to go back to California," Sarah said.

"I would have worked here for free to avoid getting roped into my dad's campaign," Emily said. "Helping out at the B and B was a perfect solution. We had a full house."

Blake set down a tablet-size computer screen on the counter as he poured himself a mug of coffee. "I would have guessed that winter was your busy season, with the skiing."

"Not at all," Sarah said as she laid out the fixings for a ham-and-cheese sandwich. Her earlier clumsiness was forgotten as she deftly sliced bread and tomato. "Most skiers stay in hotels that are closer to the slopes. The people who come here are usually interested in day trips, hiking, bicycling and sightseeing. I'm busiest in summer and in fall when the aspen leaves turn gold."

While she assembled his plate with a sandwich and an apple, they all three chatted. Emily quickly ate her muffin and excused herself so she could get ready for the arrival of her groom and the general.

Sarah and Blake ended up in the dining room that connected to the kitchen through a swinging door. She sat at the head of the long table that had been in her family for as long as she could remember, and he was to her right.

"Tell me about this place," he said. "How did you get to be an innkeeper?"

"Are you asking what a nice girl like me is doing in a place like this?"

He raised a skeptical eyebrow. "I don't remember calling you a nice girl."

"Never mind." She didn't want to hear his opinion of her. "Being an innkeeper is in my blood. My ancestor Prudence Hanover settled in Carbondale in the mid-1800s and ran a boardinghouse for miners. She'd lost her husband in the Civil War and never remarried, but she had four kids with a mysterious lover."

The lover turned out to be the infamous Louis Rousseau, who had a whole other family on the other side of the mountain. The dashing Frenchman was a charming cad, and Prudence was a smart businesswoman who made a good living with her boardinghouse.

"After Prudence passed away, one of her daughters took over the family business, then another generation. In the early 1900s, another daughter—Trudy Bentley—bought this place and refurbished it as a hunting lodge."

"You mentioned Theodore Roosevelt," he said.

"He visited Colorado frequently when he was setting up national parks," she said. "Teddy had his flaws, but he was an environmentalist. When he was in this area, he stayed at Bentley's B and B. We had lots of other famous people who came here to relax. One of the walls in my office is covered with photographs of celebrities."

"You're proud of the B and B." He was devouring his sandwich in huge bites, and she wondered if one ham-and-cheese would be enough to satisfy his appetite.

"My family has done a lot of work on the place, adding on and renovating and repairing. My big contribution has been the trail markers—burnt wood signs showing easy hiking trails in the area."

"Your parents?"

"They pretty much left me in charge eight years ago when they moved to California and enrolled in college." She thought back to those early years and shuddered. "It wasn't easy being the boss. That's when I hired Emily, which turned out to be a brilliant move. Her easygoing attitude is what kept me sane."

"You love what you do."

She knew how lucky she was. Some people never found a lifestyle and occupation that made them happy. For her, the B and B came ready-made. "I like running this place, and I do a good job. It's pretty much perfect."

"You wouldn't change a thing," he said.

"I've got no complaints." There was, however, a glaring hole in her perfect B and B bubble. Like so many Bentley women before her, Sarah was alone. Though her mother had been an exception, falling in love with her father and raising Sarah and her brother, her mother fit the mold of a strong, independent woman. She'd refused to change her family name and insisted on staying at the B and B until Sarah was old enough to take over. It hadn't been a surprise when her mom decided on law school.

Glancing across the table at Blake, she couldn't believe how much she was talking. Hospitality was all about the guest, and Sarah usually sat back and listened while others chatted. "Enough about me."

"I want to hear more," he said. "This is just starting to get interesting."

"Really? You didn't think the legend about the mystery Frenchman was intriguing? He was supposed to have a lost treasure."

"I want to hear about you, your story."

He pinned her with his sharp, blue-eyed gaze. And she felt like he could see through her defenses to the core of her loneliness, the fear that she wasn't meant to find a mate and would live her life alone at the B and B. Not that it was a bad life.

Her work with the Forest Preservation Society fulfilled her, and she was constantly busy.

His gaze invited her to share her truth, but she wasn't ready. She cleared her throat. "Give me the update on the security plans."

"I talked to Jeremy this morning. He's been monitoring chatter about the general and hasn't heard anything about a kidnap attempt. I'm hoping that the failure was enough to discourage another try."

Not exactly a solid reassurance. "What about Kovak's investigation?"

"He's still digging through records from rental car places and checking hotel registries. We don't have a name to go on. So this is a lot of guesswork. As for Farley and his friends, they don't know anything."

"We're stuck at zero?"

Blake picked up his coffee mug and shrugged. "Forewarned is forearmed."

Four-armed? She imagined a Hindu goddess with extra limbs, even though she knew that wasn't what he meant. "Because we know there's a threat, we can be prepared. Like you said, four-armed."

He picked up the tablet-size computer screen and passed it to her. "This shows the feed from four different cameras. Give it a swipe, and it shows four more directions."

She checked out the black-and-white views that

showed the approach road and the area surrounding the B and B. Tree branches bobbed in the wind. A glob of snow fell from a high point. In one view, she saw a bull elk with a six-point rack of antlers. "Very cool."

"I can transfer these views onto your computer or even a phone," he said. "At night, the cameras switch to infrared vision."

With this kind of surveillance, it would be difficult for anyone to sneak up on them. "The Reuben twins are going to love this. I told them to come back tonight so they could help out."

"Good thinking. Even with the cameras, nothing beats an actual guard standing watch. They hear things, sense changes in atmosphere and see things a camera doesn't notice."

He spoke with the voice of experience. He'd been trained for this kind of work, and she appreciated his skill. "I want to thank you," she said, "for making the wedding possible. Emily really has her heart set on this ceremony."

"I'm glad it worked out." He rose from his seat and stood behind her, watching the display on the screens. "I like it here. I wanted to stay."

When he reached past her shoulder to swipe the screen, she felt the warmth of his body and caught a whiff of a woodsy aroma. Her eyelids closed in a prolonged blink, and she allowed herself to enjoy his nearness.

"I'm glad, too."

Her voice was a whisper, more intimate than she'd intended. Being close to him was intoxicating. She needed to be careful before she did something that she regretted.

Chapter Seven

By the time Jeremy and General Charles Hamilton were expected to arrive, Sarah had done her prep work in the kitchen and the spaghetti sauce was bubbling, filling the house with a spicy aroma. She'd checked the bedrooms to make sure everything was in order and fielded several phone calls from the wedding caterers, the florist and the cake baker. With all of the other potential disasters looming, it seemed that the February weather might be turning into a problem. Though today was clear and sunny, heavy snow was in the forecast for Friday, and the people providing the food for the wedding were beginning to worry. If the snow started tomorrow, Thursday, they would drop things off ahead of time.

Standing at the front window, she watched as a silver rental SUV parked in front of the B and B. "They're here."

In a flash of denim and a lacy blouse, Emily ran across the room, flung open the front door, dashed across the porch and flew into her husband-to-be's waiting arms. Jeremy scooped her off the ground and spun her around in a circle.

Stepping outside onto the porch, Sarah couldn't help beaming. The sheer joy radiating from Jeremy and Emily was contagious, but not powerful enough to infect the unsmiling general, who emerged from the front passenger seat.

"What a grump," she murmured under her breath.

"You're mistaken," Blake said quietly as he joined her on the porch. "That's his happy face."

She glanced toward him. He'd shaved in honor of the general's arrival. With the grungy beard gone, she noticed the sharp angle of his jaw and the fullness of his lower lip, the kind of lip that begged to be kissed. Reining in her thoughts, she said, "You look good."

"So do you."

"Thanks." She'd made an effort, putting on makeup and brushing her hair to a warm shine. Instead of her usual jeans, she wore gray leggings and a teal shirt under a long cardigan that fell halfway down her thighs in back.

Since none of the men—not even the two aides—were in uniform, Blake didn't salute as he descended the stairs from the porch and shook the general's hand. In spite of the casual jackets, their greeting had an air of military formality.

"General," Blake said, "this is Sarah Bentley, the owner of the B and B."

The general's herringbone tweed jacket had been tailored to fit his very square, very straight shoulders. His pure white hair gleamed in the late afternoon sun, and the lines of his face looked like they'd been carved from oak. His voice rumbled in his chest as he said, "Pleased to meet you, Sarah."

She gripped his hand firmly. "The pleasure is mine..." No way was she going to spend the next four days calling this man General. "Charles."

His white eyebrows lifted a fraction of an inch.

She continued, "Do you prefer Chuck?"

"Emily didn't tell me much about you."

Emily was noticing right now. Behind the general's back, she was making frantic throat-cutting gestures to get Sarah to shut up. *Fat chance.* The general might be in charge of a battalion of bureaucrats at the Pentagon, but he was in her house now. And she was the boss. If her light teasing offended him, she didn't really care. After this weekend, she'd never see the man again.

She smiled into the older man's chiseled face. "Maybe I should call you Chuckie."

"Charles will be fine."

"Great, come on inside and let me show you around."

With the general and his two aides—Maddox and Alvardo—in tow, she gave the grand tour from the left wing of the house where the game room, library and her office were located to the upstairs where she had given General Hamilton the suite with the bathroom. His aides had bedrooms across the hall.

"We don't have room service," she said. "If you're hungry during the night, you have to jog down to the kitchen and help yourself."

The general strode across the room to the pine bedside table. His posture was so rigid that he seemed to creak as he bent at the waist and picked up the telephone receiver. "If there's no room service, why do you have a phone?"

"It's an extension to call out," she said. "Cell phone service is spotty here."

"Not anymore," Blake said as he reached into the pocket of his jacket and took out two phones. He gave one to the general and the other to Mike Alvardo. "Satellite phones, totally reliable."

"Unless there's a blizzard," she said with a devilish flutter of her lashes. "Or a bear knocks over the satellite terminal."

"Not likely," he muttered. "The terminal is halfway up a tree."

"Bears climb."

The general barked a laugh, and they all turned to stare. It would have been less startling if a hundred-year-old spruce jumped out of the forest and started break dancing.

He laughed again. "I like you, Sarah."

"Same here, Charles."

"Your B and B is delightful," he said, "but we haven't seen all of it."

"Is there something you're looking for?"

"Where's your bedroom?"

Well, well, aren't you the dirty old man? "Downstairs. And I keep my door locked."

"Wise decision." He charged across the room, taking command. "Let's go downstairs to the big room with the fireplace and discuss the current situation. FYI, Blake, I don't believe any of it. My enemies are devious, but they aren't fools. There's no logical reason for them to kidnap Emily."

DOWNSTAIRS, BLAKE POSITIONED himself across the room from the fireplace. He was plenty warm. The general's last comment had him sweating. Blake agreed that the attack on Emily was neither well planned nor well executed, but the threat was real. The last thing he needed was to foster an attitude of complacency among the wedding guests. They needed to be on their guard.

He waited for everyone to get settled after they served themselves coffee or tea from a setup on the dining room table. There were also two trays of snacks. One was veggies, and the other chocolate chip cookies. Nobody touched the carrots.

Jeremy and Emily had pretty much tuned out everyone else. They snuggled together on the sofa, whispering and staring at each other with greedy eyes.

Of the two aides, Alvardo was taller, more self-composed and probably higher in rank. In a show of efficiency, he'd brought his leather attaché case with him and placed it on the floor beside the rocking chair where he sat with both feet planted firmly on the floor to keep the chair from moving. His build was solid, and his blond hair was military-cut. For the details regarding the threat, Blake knew he'd be consulting with Alvardo.

That wasn't a bad place to start. He approached the rocking chair and leaned down. "Jeremy sent me an email list of people who had a beef with the general. Can you give me more detailed information?"

"Whatever you need." He lowered his voice. "What's the deal with Sarah?"

"Are you asking for yourself or the old man?"

Alvardo winked. "The general likes to flirt, but I'm the one who wants to know."

"She's single," Blake said, "and I saw her first."

He turned to the other aide, Maddox, and gave him one of the screens showing the views outside the B and B. "If you notice anything suspicious, let me know."

Maddox nodded. “Yes, sir.”

The general sat in a leather wingback chair and placed his coffee mug on the table beside him. “All right, Blake. Give us your briefing.”

Years of military experience had taught him how to quickly sketch in the outlines of a situation without raising too many questions. He covered the events of the previous night in fewer than five minutes and was about to proceed to the plans for investigating when the general interrupted.

“A question,” he said. “Did the kidnapper attempt to disguise his voice on the telephone?”

“He had no reason to,” Blake said. “He thought he was talking to the man he’d hired.”

“If you heard his voice again, would you recognize it?”

“I believe so.” There had been nothing unusual about the voice. No regional accent. No unusual pitch. “Do you have samples of voices I can listen to?”

Alvardo answered, “All conversations coming into the general’s office are routinely recorded. I can get copies of those calls sent to your computer.”

Blake imagined himself sitting for hours listening to mundane telephone calls. “When we have the suspects narrowed down, that could come in handy.”

Determining the suspects would be tedious

work. He explained that Deputy Kovak would be coming for dinner tonight and bringing the information he'd gathered from the rental car companies and the local hotels. They would compare those names with the lists of people who had a grudge against the general.

"That's a lot of names," the general said. "I'm taking the heat for closing down several military institutions and canceling orders for equipment. People will be put out of work. Their salaries will be cut. They're mad. And, to tell you the truth, I don't blame them."

"Their anger is misdirected," Alvardo said. "The death threats should be going to the idiots in Congress who cut the budget in the first place."

"I'm sure they are," Emily piped up. "People don't hesitate before blasting Congress."

"Moving on," Blake said before they could get embroiled in a political discussion. "General, have any of these threats focused on you personally?"

"You bet they have."

Alvardo reached down and patted his briefcase. "I can show you emails calling the general every name in the book and telling him in detail what they'd do if they met him. There are photographs of him with devil horns, a pitchfork and a spiked tail."

"The people who yell and scream don't worry me," the general said as he leaned forward in his chair. "It's those sneaky bastards. The ones who sit back and silently curse my name—the psychopaths."

Blake wasn't a profiler, but he thought psychopath might be an accurate description. He added, "This individual isn't passive. He's taking action."

"And he's not a downtrodden minimum-wage worker," Sarah said as she moved away from the coffee urn and stood near the fireplace. "He had enough money to get here and to rent a vehicle, not to mention the three thousand bucks he paid Farley."

"He's clever enough to uncover inside information." Blake remembered how the kidnapper had known his name. "We can't dismiss the kidnapper as a pathetic lunatic."

"However," the general said, "his scheme is deeply flawed. He planned to kidnap Emily, believing he could use her as blackmail to make me do what he wanted."

"What's the flaw?" Sarah asked.

"As soon as Emily was released, I could reverse my decision."

Blake had come to a similar conclusion and had been considering alternatives. "He might have been planning to ask for a ransom. Or he was showing you that he could attack at any time, planting the seeds of fear."

"I know the sick rationalizations for kidnapping," the general said. "I was stationed in the Middle East for nearly ten years."

"Yes, sir."

"By all means, continue with the investigation as planned, but I think we're going to find out that the kidnapping doesn't have anything to do with budgets or logic or with me."

Sarah picked up the poker and adjusted the logs in the fireplace. The flames picked out red highlights in her hair. "What are you implying, Charles?"

"There was another motive. Hatred. Revenge. Jealousy. This person wanted to hurt or to frighten Emily."

Blake glanced over at the happy couple on the sofa. Jeremy held her close. His fingers laced through hers. This should have been a blissful time for them, waiting to share their vows and start a life together. Though he hated to add to their troubles, he needed to be thorough. "We should widen the scope of our investigation."

"Don't forget Emily's father," the general said.

She tore free from Jeremy's embrace and leaped to her feet. "You've been waiting for a chance to blame him."

"Your father is a public figure. He has enemies."

"Daddy would never do anything to put me in danger."

"Neither would I," the general said.

Blake was about to step between them, but Sarah moved more quickly. Her alto voice was calm and soothing. "We're all friends here. There's no reason for us to snipe at each other. The important thing is to find the bad guy and get him out of the way before the wedding."

Blake joined her. "Jeremy and Emily, I want you to sit down with Sarah and make a list of people who might want to hurt you."

"Why?" Emily demanded.

"The wedding could be a trigger. The idea that you're getting married might be the last straw for a person who's already on the edge."

"Oh, please." Emily tossed her head. "Are we talking about former boyfriends?"

"Or girlfriends," Sarah said as she hooked arms with her friend. "There might be some crazy young lady who hired a kidnapper to keep her darling Jeremy Hamilton from getting hitched."

The general laughed again. "I certainly do enjoy you, Sarah."

"You gentlemen stay out here," she said. "I'll take Emily and Jeremy to my office. Dinner is at six so don't fill up on cookies."

While she ushered Emily and Jeremy down the hall, Blake moved to a brown leather chair opposite the general, who was still baring his teeth in a grin. "That Sarah, she's a pistol, isn't she?"

The smile didn't reach the general's gunmetal-gray eyes, and his casual posture didn't hide his stiff shoulders or the corded muscles in his throat. An unseen pressure squeezed him tightly, and he was doing his best to hang on to control.

Though Blake had never served under General Hamilton, he was familiar with the reputation of this man who had been an important part of the command structure in Afghanistan. He was known for his dedication to his troops, and his ability to make quick decisions.

The general avoided his gaze by tasting his coffee. "Jeremy tells me that you're planning to retire."

"I am."

"You're kind of young to opt out."

"It's time," Blake said. "I liked being a ranger. The work suited me, and I felt like I was making a difference. But I'm tired of war, ready for a change."

"With your background, you could get a decent military job in the States. I'd give you a recommendation."

"Thank you, sir. But I want to explore my options."

"Riding a desk isn't for everyone." The general rubbed at his forehead. "Sometimes, I wonder if coming back to D.C. was the right decision for me. Every morning when I wake up in my king-size bed and get suited up in my uniform, I wish I was wearing fatigues and stepping out of a tent."

Blake glanced over at the two aides, who were on the edges of their chairs, listening intently. He looked back at the general and said, "You're an important presence in Washington. They need to hear from somebody who's been there."

"That's why I do it. To protect my troops. Some of these bureaucratic snafus are more dangerous than IEDs." He leveraged himself out of the chair. "Let's go over to the dining room table and Alvardo can show us what he's got."

In minutes, Alvardo had spread an organized array of color-coded folders. "I have this intelligence narrowed down to a single flash drive, but it helps to see the originals."

"What do the colors mean?" Blake asked.

"Green represents survivalists and cults. Yellow stands for antiwar groups. We can pretty much disregard blue because those threats are corporate and legal. The largest group of threats—which are in the purple folder—come from workers who are losing their jobs or livelihoods."

That left the red folder.

"What's that one?" Blake asked.

"Old news from the field," Alvardo said. "Those threats are at least three years old, which is before the general was stationed at the Pentagon."

"From the field," Blake repeated, "from people whose lives were affected by military action."

"Afghani politicians, tribal chiefs, merchants who lost their businesses, grieving mothers." Alvardo rattled off the list with the casual disregard of someone who had never seen action.

"Terrorists," Blake said. He hoped they would never have to see the names in the red folder.

Chapter Eight

After an excellent spaghetti dinner, the guests at Bentley's Bed-and-Breakfast—which now included Kovak, the Pitkin County sheriff and the Reuben twins—left the dining room table and moved into the great room with the fireplace. Blake watched as they separated into factions. Jeremy and Emily were, of course, lost in their own little world. The twins and Maddox had taken responsibility for guard duty and were cheerfully synchronizing their watches, studying the infrared camera feed and parceling out weapons. Kovak and the sheriff fell deep into conversation with the general and Alvardo. Sarah was cleaning up.

Blake knew exactly where he belonged.

In the kitchen, he snatched a dish towel from the rack and approached the strawberry-blonde woman rinsing dishes at the sink. "Reporting for duty," he said.

"You should go with the others," she said. "Everything in here is under control."

"I'm staying." He wanted to be with her. Nothing else seemed to make sense. "If you don't give me a job, I'll sit on this stool and watch you work."

"Fine." She glanced at him over her shoulder. "There's a broom and dustpan in the mudroom. The floors in here could use a swipe."

Dutifully, he went to the mudroom. "That was a good rule you made for dinner. No talking about the investigation."

"My family is big on civilized conversation. My grandma used to have a sign. 'For good digestion, no talk of politics or religion will be tolerated at the dinner table.'"

"Old-fashioned values," he said as he returned with the broom.

"But practical," she said. "Bentley's started as a boardinghouse, and there needed to be rules so those miners wouldn't tear each other apart."

He could easily imagine her as a pioneer innkeeper keeping order in her house, but he was glad she dressed like a modern woman. For her kitchen chores, she'd taken off her long sweater and wore a pin-striped apron over her blouse and the leggings that outlined her shapely calves and thighs.

When they were first introduced, he'd noticed that she was an attractive woman. The more time he spent with her, the more appealing she became.

"Tonight, you were the queen, sitting at the head of the table and directing your adoring subjects."

She scoffed. "Adoring subjects?"

"Oh, yeah. The general thinks you're a pistol. Kovak trusts you with his life. Even Alvardo asked me about you."

"And what did you tell him?"

Even though Blake had gotten his nose honked, he couldn't resist teasing her. "I told him we were sleeping together."

She pivoted away from the sink and glared. "Liar."

"I saved you from being pestered by Alvardo."

"And how do you know he's not my type?" she asked. "I might be looking for an uptight guy who has a briefcase attached to his wrist."

"I didn't know you were into boredom."

She turned off the water in the sink. "I have a question for you. You said I was a queen. Why not a princess? I've always wanted to be a princess."

"Being a queen is better." He swept his way across the kitchen floor until he was standing beside her. "Princesses are silly and helpless, always needing to be rescued from dragons. That's not you."

"I guess not." She returned to her task of loading the dishwasher. "Before dinner, I heard you guys talking about suspects. Did you get the list narrowed down?"

"Not much."

So far, they hadn't found a match with people

who had threatened the general and clients of the local rental car services and major hotels. The lack of solid evidence left them discussing profiles, motives and possibilities.

Blake preferred a clear-cut mission. "There's too much speculation. With nothing to go on but badly worded threats, we're starting to think of the suspects as players in a parlor game, giving them cute nicknames like Kenny the Contractor and Stevie the Survivalist. I don't like it. It's not smart to underestimate your enemies."

"I agree." She closed the dishwasher. "Jeremy and Emily aren't taking this seriously at all."

"Did you get a list of names from them?"

She nodded. "As long as the sheriff is here, we might want to run those names through a criminal database."

"Consider it done."

They were close enough that he could see the rim of dark, rich chocolate-brown surrounding her irises. Her wide, beautiful eyes, framed by upswept brows and thick lashes, softened her angular features. In their depths, he saw the warmth and vulnerability that she kept hidden.

"If you're finished with the floor," she said, "you could put the wine bottles in the recycle bin in the mudroom."

"Why do you think Jeremy and Emily aren't concerned about the threat?"

"I don't know Jeremy all that well," she said, "but Emily doesn't like to go negative. She wants to pretend that the whole world is sweetness and light."

"You don't agree."

"If the kidnap attempt had been successful," she said, "I think Emily would have been hurt. How could the kidnapper let her go free when she could identify him?"

"In the Middle East, kidnappings aren't uncommon. Family members are taken for ransom or as a threat, and they're often released unharmed."

"We're in Colorado," she reminded him. "Aspen might not have a military presence, but our police are pretty good at finding people when there's a witness."

He thought of the red folder. The general had enemies outside the borders of the United States. "Why Emily? Why would they go after her?"

"Well, she is kind of a princess."

"Prone to attack by dragons and other nefarious beings."

"Absolutely."

Looking up at him, she flashed a bright smile and the lightness of it reflected in her eyes. Though tempted, he didn't move any closer to her. Having his nose honked once was enough.

She stepped away from him and reached behind her back to untie her long apron. When she cast aside the pin-striped apron and adjusted the collar on her blouse, he was struck by the contrast between the rich teal fabric and her milky skin. A tiny, heart-shaped gold locket nestled in the hollow of her throat.

His fingers itched to caress her, and he actually stuffed his hands into the pockets of his jeans to keep from reaching out and tracing the path of the delicate gold chain that encircled her neck. As she crossed the kitchen to hang her apron on a peg near the door, he watched her athletic stride and unconsciously graceful gestures. Being alone with her might be a mistake. If so, it was an error in judgment he intended to make repeatedly.

Unaware of the effect she was having on him, she said, "You had a theory that made a lot of sense."

"What was that?"

"The wedding could be the trigger."

He focused on her lips as she spoke. "Explain."

"One of Emily's former boyfriends could have been fantasizing about her for years. When he hears about the wedding, something snaps." She snapped her fingers to illustrate. "And he turns into a total crazy person."

"Crazy person?"

"That's probably not an FBI profiler term, but you know what I mean."

"Does anybody on Jeremy and Emily's list fit that description?"

"I don't know." She shrugged inside her long sweater that covered up way too much of her body. "Let's get started on researching that criminal database and see what we can find."

He didn't want to share his time with Sarah, but the investigation demanded their attention. It was all a balancing act. Caution versus paranoia. Desire weighed against practical concerns.

IN HER OFFICE, Kovak and Alvardo had stationed themselves at the two desks and flipped open their laptops. They were the officials who had access to the restricted criminal databases, and neither wanted to share. As they explained, Sarah was impressed and kind of creeped out by the depth and scope of their records. According to Kovak and Alvardo, almost anyone with an arrest record or a court action was fair game.

"That doesn't seem right," she said.

"Computers," said Alvardo, "are the best thing that ever happened to law enforcement."

"What about the right to privacy?"

"When you get arrested, you lose that right."

Outside the windows of the B and B, the wind kicked up, bringing the snow that had been forecast closer. Inside the office, bits and bytes of information danced across the computer screens to form photographs and data.

An embarrassing mug shot of Sarah's face—with haystack hair and unfocused eyes—appeared on the screen of Kovak's computer. She would have liked to say it was her evil twin. No such luck.

Kovak looked up at her. "Malicious mischief?"

"It was over ten years ago," she explained. "I was in college in Boulder and I set off some illegal fireworks."

"Most of the time," the deputy said, "the officer wouldn't bother booking somebody for such a minor offense."

She winced. "I might have made a smart-aleck comment."

"Yeah, that would do it."

Emily leaned over Kovak's shoulder. "Do me."

Her fiancé chuckled as he placed his hand on her slender waist. "I can't believe you have a criminal record."

Sarah remembered her conversation in the forest with Emily when she'd said that she and Jeremy agreed to disagree on some issues. Poor Jeremy was in for some big surprises.

Emily's mug shot was perky and adorable. She could have been posing for a magazine cover. There were two charges of disturbing the peace. "Protests," she said. "Let's not tell your father."

He nodded agreement. "Let's not."

"I think it's admirable," Blake said. "Somebody's got to stand up and save the endangered ferrets."

"And the wolverines," Sarah added as she plopped down on the plaid sofa beside him.

His long legs stretched out in front of him as he slouched against the sofa cushions and rested a blue-and-yellow-striped coffee mug on his lap. His eyelids drooped at half-mast. "Who's the number one person on your list, Jeremy?"

"That would be Teresa Bonanno. Actually, her father—Carl Bonanno—is the problem. After we broke up, he came to see me and ask me to give her another chance."

"Of course he did," Emily purred. "You're a catch."

"He said he wanted an army man for his little girl. It was four years ago, and he still sends me a Christmas card."

A search for Teresa turned up nothing. Her father was a different story. Papa Bonanno owned a pawn shop in Cicero, had served a term in prison as a young man and had a list of arrests for fraud and robbery. "Nothing violent," Kovak noted.

"Which doesn't mean he couldn't hire somebody if he really wanted to stop the wedding," Blake said. "Can we check his whereabouts?"

Kovak jotted a note. "I'll do it tomorrow."

"Here's a live one," Alvardo said. "A contractor who stands to lose millions if his government-funded projects are shut down. He has a temper. His criminal record includes two assault charges. He got off on both of them."

"Which means he also has a good lawyer," Kovak said.

Sarah didn't see the connection. "Why would this contractor care if Jeremy and Emily get married?"

Alvardo shrugged. "He wouldn't."

"Then why come after Emily?"

"Because he mistakenly thought he could grab her and get away with it." Alvardo gave her a grin. "He wasn't counting on your quick thinking in making an escape."

"Sliding down the mountain on my butt?"

"An ace maneuver," Blake said.

As they went through several other names, her interest waned. The tracking down of criminals was nowhere near as exciting as it appeared in detective shows. The process seemed to be a lot of digging through information that would yield more areas to dig through. They could spend the whole night here and not get any closer to a solution.

"Time for me to go to sleep," she said as she rose to her feet. "Breakfast tomorrow is whenever you wake up. Just come down to the kitchen, and I'll fix you something."

Blake set down his coffee mug and stood. "I'll walk you down the hall."

Though she didn't need an escort in her own house, she didn't object to his gentlemanly offer. In the living room, she noticed that someone had put another log on the fireplace. They didn't need the heat, and she was a little concerned about leaving the flames burning so high. The general and the sheriff appeared to be deep in conversation, both men sipping single malt whiskey from heavy-bottomed tumblers. The general started to get out of his chair when she entered, but she gestured for him to stay seated.

"Have a good night's sleep," she said.

"I appreciate your hospitality, Sarah."

"Thank you, Charles."

Outside the door to her room, Blake hesitated. "Don't worry," he said, "I'll make sure the fire is okay before I go to bed."

"How did you know I was worried?"

"I can read you like a book."

"And I thought I was a woman of mystery."

"Afraid not." He leaned against the wall beside her door with his arms folded across his chest. "I can tell what's going on inside that pretty little head."

"Yeah?" She stared into his face. "What am I thinking right now?"

He widened his eyes, pretending to see into her

thoughts. Then he gave a slow nod. "The answer is yes."

Once again, he was teasing her. She didn't want to like these games he played, but she couldn't help smiling nor could she stop the warm blush she felt spreading from her throat to her cheeks. "If the answer is yes, what was the question?"

"Should we kiss?"

He unfolded one arm and rested it on her shoulder, guiding her closer to him. She had plenty of time to slip from his grasp or honk his nose or walk away. Consciously, she hadn't been thinking about a kiss, but as soon as he spoke, she knew the idea had been playing in the back of her mind all night. Should they kiss? Would they?

"Yes," she whispered.

His mouth pressed firmly against hers, taking control. With one hand, he held her shoulder. The other rested at her waist inside her sweater. His fingertips slid up her rib cage to the curve of her breast. A gush of liquid heat flooded her senses. Her heart jumped as her pulse went into high gear.

Her lips slipped against his, tasting and demanding. She caught his full lower lip in her teeth and pulled, teasing him. And he responded forcefully, kissing her hard and using his tongue to push inside.

And when he pulled away, she felt like she'd

never really been kissed before. Everything until now had been practice.

Blake was the real deal.

Chapter Nine

The next morning, Sarah was—as usual—up at daybreak. The breakfast part of bed-and-breakfast meant she needed to provide something to eat for her guests, and her intention was to make fresh muffins. As usual, she stumbled around the kitchen half-asleep. *Need coffee, I need coffee now.* She went through the brewing process and waited—as usual—for the coffee to drip into the glass carafe.

In spite of the familiar routine, she didn't feel like her everyday self. Outside the windows, dawn scoured the cloudy skies with crimson and maroon. What was that old saying? *Red sky at morning, sailors take warning.* The snow was coming; there was more trouble on the horizon.

She should have been worried about the weather and the kidnap attempt and her guests and the million things that needed to be done before the wedding. Instead, she felt an *unusual* sense of anticipation. Her heart was light. Her feet wanted to dance. She turned on the streaming satellite radio, which had been tuned by Emily to a pop station, and heard Taylor Swift. Sarah's moccasins tapped in time to the beat.

As a practical woman, she knew better than to make too much of one kiss, even a very excellent kiss. She shouldn't forget that Blake was only going to be here for a few days—not long enough to establish a relationship. But nobody said she had to be serious.

For once in her life, she could have a wild, crazy, passionate fling with a big, strong guy. There didn't seem to be a choice. He wouldn't get out of her head. Her dreams last night had been X-rated, and Blake played a starring role in every one.

She was reaching for the carafe when the Reuben twins tromped through the kitchen door.

"I told you I smelled coffee," John Reuben said. "Hi, Sarah. What's with the music?"

"Apparently, Taylor Swift is never ever ever going to get back together."

"Her loss," John said.

Sarah poured herself a cup of coffee. "Any problems last night?"

"Nothing at all." The other twin, William, placed the computer screen with the camera views on the countertop. "We spent a lot of time talking to Blake."

So had she, but her time had been romantic dream whisperings. "What did you talk about?"

"Signing up for the military."

"We could see the world." John flung his arms wide. His wingspan from fingertip to fingertip was over six feet. "I always wanted to go to Japan, where they have ninjas and those big, fat wrestlers."

William nodded quietly as he poured himself a mug of coffee.

The twins were identical in appearance but so different in temperament that she never had trouble telling them apart. William was thoughtful and soft-spoken while his brother was bursting with energy. John was a few minutes older and liked to be first at everything.

Though Sarah was only about ten years older than the twins, she'd watched them grow up and felt motherly toward them. Joining the army was a big decision and shouldn't be made because they happened to meet a ranger who was a super-cool role model. "William, I thought you were going to college."

"I can still do that, and the military gives me benefits that will help with the tuition."

"We might as well enlist," John said. "It's hard to find a job around here. Dad can't afford for us to work with him full-time at the hardware store, even if we are the best handymen in the county."

"You have a job here until after the wedding," she said.

"We're doing security." John puffed up his chest. "Do you really think anybody is going to attack the B and B?"

"Don't know, but I'd rather be safe than sorry. I want you guys to come back every night until Sunday."

Although she hadn't heard an identifiable sound, her ears pricked up. She sensed Blake's approach. The homey kitchen atmosphere seemed charged with energy. A shaft of light shone through the window like a spotlight as he entered.

His hair was still wet and spiky from the shower. The sharp line of his jaw was clean-shaven. And his eyes, his incredible blue eyes, glistened. She wanted to say something clever to show that she wasn't completely disarmed, but her mouth was too busy gaping. She shoved the coffee mug to her lips and took a gulp. *Caffeine, don't fail me now.* "Good morning, Blake."

"Back at you." He greeted the twins and poured himself a mug of coffee.

She hadn't planned on seeing him this early. Didn't the man ever sleep late? If she'd known he'd be up, she would have gotten dressed instead of stumbling around in pink plaid pajamas and an ancient blue bathrobe. "I just came down here to get my muffins started."

"I'd be happy to help with your muffins."

Why did that sound so sexy? "I'm happy if you're happy."

"We had a phone call last night from Emily's dad," he said. "It seems that the senator is into conspiracy theories."

She didn't know Emily's parents well but remembered a very long evening drinking craft beer with the senator and hearing every detail about the mysterious Area 51 in Nevada. "I hate to ask, but what does the senator think about the kidnap attempt?"

"I think we ruled out aliens," Blake said.

"Wow!" John Reuben's eyes popped wide. "Aliens?"

"I'm joking," Blake said.

"Yeah, right. I knew that."

"The bad news," Blake said, "is that the senator has enough suspects to populate a midsize mountain town. The less bad news is that he doesn't consider any of them to be violent."

She didn't quite believe that reasoning. "A kidnapping at gunpoint isn't violent?"

Blake shrugged. "He's adamant about having the wedding proceed as planned. He made quite a speech about not negotiating with bad guys and not letting them dictate his course of action."

She was wide-awake enough to read between the lines. "Long story short," she said, "the senator thinks the threat is all about him and he won't back down. The general sees only his own enemies. It's a clear case of dueling egos."

"You don't much like these guys."

"Not true," she said as she took another dose of caffeine. "They both have fine qualities, and I really like the senator's wife, Rebecca. I just wish we could eliminate any possible danger before the wedding."

William Reuben held up the screen showing the camera feeds. "Hey, look at this. There's a van coming down the road."

"Are you expecting anyone?" Blake asked her.

"Not until later today."

Blake straightened his shoulders, stepped away from the counter and faced the twins. With a subtle shift in posture, he took on an attitude of authority. "Gentlemen, we need to identify the driver and passengers in the vehicle. Use caution."

Sarah followed them to the front room, where she stood at the window to watch. To her surprise, the twins moved with the sort of mature assurance and discipline they might learn in basic training. Blake must have been working with them. On the porch, he made a couple of quick gestures. William took a position at the edge of the porch with his rifle aimed at the approaching van. John went left and stood behind her truck.

Blake descended from the porch. His right hand

rested on the butt of the handgun holstered at his hip. Until this moment, Sarah hadn't noticed he was armed. He was an intimidating presence as he approached the vehicle.

A skinny guy with tight jeans and a fringed leather jacket emerged from the driver's side. He flapped his arms like an angry crow as he talked to Blake.

She squinted through the window. The guy didn't look familiar, and she hadn't made any reservations for this weekend. Had Bentley's B and B turned into a problem magnet?

When Blake waved to her, she opened the front door and peeked out. "What is it?"

"Ollie and the Dewdrops," Blake said. "He says they're a band."

She remembered—a guitar, a violin and a flute. They'd played at some romantic event Emily and Jeremy had attended, and Emily had been trying to book them. Though Sarah was glad the band could make it, today was Thursday and the wedding wasn't until Saturday. "They're a little early."

The guy in the fringed jacket waved to her. "Our other gig is over. We've got no place to stay."

And why did that make Ollie and the Dewdrops her problem? A gust of wind rattled the treetops, reminding her of the impending blizzard that was supposed to start tomorrow. She had to plan for heavy snow, had to make sure there was enough food and had to check on the flowers. Her day was getting more and more complicated.

For one irresponsible moment, she wondered what would happen if she told everybody to back off while she dragged Blake into her bedroom and had her way with him.

The urge passed, somewhat to her chagrin.

AFTER BLAKE HAD gotten Ollie and his two Dewdrop pals settled in the twelve-bed dormitory area on the third floor of the B and B, he collected their driver's licenses. Checking identification for every person who joined the wedding party was a necessary security measure.

On the second floor, he tapped on the door to the bedroom that had been assigned to Maddox and Alvardo. The senior officer answered quickly. Alvardo wore an army sweat suit with a black knit cap covering his close-cropped blond hair. His complexion was ruddy, and he looked pumped.

"Been out for a run?" Blake asked.

"Five miles every day." He slipped into the hall and closed the bedroom door behind him as though he had something to hide. "Can I help you?"

"I need your computer skills. During the weekend, we're going to have civilians coming and going."

His light eyebrows pinched into a disapproving frown. "This B and B is supposed to be a secure location."

"It's only as secure as we make it," Blake said. "I want you to check IDs. See if you can work out something with Kovak to use the law enforcement database."

"I don't need Kovak. I can access any damn intelligence I need. How deep should I go with background?"

"Flag anything suspicious. Bring it to me, and we'll talk about it."

Blake didn't completely trust this guy. Alvardo was an ambitious political officer who probably hadn't seen a lot of action. Though Blake didn't judge a man by his combat missions, he appreciated the sense of teamwork that came from working with a squad in the field. If push came to shove, he wasn't sure Alvardo would have his back.

But he didn't have much choice. Blake handed over the driver's licenses. "You can start with these three. They're a band, and they're going to be here for the ceremony."

"A band, huh?" Alvardo tapped the licenses in his hand. "Are we going to have a bachelor party for Jeremy?"

"Tomorrow night. I'm supposed to be planning it," Blake said sheepishly. He hadn't given a thought to the bachelor party. "I guess I should hire a stripper."

"I'll do it," Alvardo readily volunteered.

"Thanks. You might check with Dolly, one of the owners at the Laughing Dog Saloon."

He hustled downstairs where a buffet was arranged on the side table in the dining room. In addition to freshly made muffins, there was fruit, cereal and yogurt. One chafing dish held breakfast burritos of scrambled eggs and chorizo. A Crock-Pot was filled with green chili. It was a decent spread, and Sarah had put it together in less than an hour.

The general sat at the foot of the table, chatting with Jeremy and Emily. The Reuben twins were walking toward the front door with Maddox.

Jeremy waved to him. "Blake, come sit."

"In a minute."

He charged through the swinging door to the kitchen where he hoped to find Sarah alone. Last night when they'd kissed, he'd felt something deeper and stronger than the sensual attraction. Not that the sexuality was lacking; he'd been on fire. But the sense of connection was too powerful to ignore.

He called it an instinct. For most of his life, he'd been a man of action who didn't spend much time analyzing and reflecting. His instincts told him who to trust. He knew without thinking when he was in danger, when to attack, when to retreat. Their kiss made his heart beat faster and his legs go weak. She was special. He needed a chance to spend some time with her, to get to know her better.

In the kitchen, he watched as she chopped a tomato on the cutting board while talking on the landline telephone and stretching the cord. The oven timer went off. She dropped the knife, grabbed an oven mitt, flipped open the oven door and pulled out another tray of muffins. Then she was back at the cutting board. Though she whirled through the kitchen like a Roller Derby queen, her phone voice was calm and her manner not frazzled.

When she hung up the phone, she glanced toward him. "What is it, Blake?"

"You've got a regular juggling act going on here."

"Nothing I can't handle," she said.

"Slow down." He couldn't talk to her while she was zooming around the kitchen.

She came to an abrupt halt and turned to him with her fists on her hips. "What do you need?"

He wanted to tell her that their kiss last night hadn't been a mistake. Holding her in his arms might have been the start of something important. He wanted to know if she felt the same way about him.

He needed another kiss.

But now wasn't the right time. Here wasn't the right place.

Chapter Ten

Blake hooked his index finger into the front bib of her striped apron and gave a little tug, pulling her toward him. Her head tilted back as though she was resisting him, but her smile was pure enticement. Before taking the last step into his arms, she untied her apron and slipped out of it, leaving him with a handful of pin-striped fabric.

"An update," he said. "The band is settled on the third floor."

"Good."

"Sometime soon, I want you to give me a tour of the trails around the house."

She returned to the countertop and started taking fresh-from-the-oven muffins from their tin and arranging them on a plate. "That can be arranged."

He watched as she bustled through the kitchen. Though she was wearing hiking boots, her step was light. Her pastel-green turtleneck was tucked into her jeans, and the sleeves were pushed up to her elbows. He asked, "When did you find time to get dressed?"

"Throwing on a pair of jeans doesn't take much effort."

"Maybe not for you," he said, "but I've worked with female troops who could spend an hour combing their hair and putting on camo fatigues."

"What can I say? I'm low maintenance."

Though he wasn't an expert, he could tell that she wasn't using any kind of makeup, and her hair was snatched into a quick ponytail. She didn't need maintenance to look good.

Before he could move toward her again, Jeremy came into the kitchen. "Great breakfast, Sarah."

"Thanks. Am I running low on anything?"

"Not that I can tell." He turned to Blake. "I understand you had some excitement this morning."

"Ollie and the Dewdrops showed up." Blake focused back on the immediate security concerns. "I need info from both of you. How many people are going to be staying here on the weekend?"

"The Reuben twins," Sarah said, "and I just got off the phone with a woman who helps me out during the busy season. She and a friend of hers are going to come over and handle the basic cooking and cleaning, but they won't be staying."

"Are they your only staff?"

"During the summer and fall I have a couple of

live-in people. Otherwise, I can handle the business by myself and with a couple of part-timers."

"Who else?" he asked.

"The senator, his wife and a speech writer," she said. "I didn't book any other guests because I wanted the families to have their privacy."

He glanced at Jeremy. "Have you and Emily invited anybody?"

"We started to," he said, "but the list got longer and more complicated. We're sticking to immediate family and both of you."

For a wedding, there weren't many people in attendance, but Blake felt crowded. Everywhere he turned, there was someone pushing into his space—a space he wanted to share with Sarah alone. "What about people who will be dropping things off?"

"Let me think." Sarah started ticking them off on her fingers. "Later today, the florist will bring roses. The wedding cake baker should be here late tonight or early tomorrow. The caterer is coming tomorrow and will be bringing two servers, and they'll be back for the ceremony on Saturday. Why do you need to know all this?"

"Background checks," he said. He'd have to set up a procedure with Alvardo to verify the people providing services before they entered the premises. "I'll need names and phone numbers for all the people coming here."

"Good thinking," Jeremy said. "Anyone could be a hired assassin."

"Not Ollie and the Dewdrops," she said as she went to the CD player. "You've got to listen to this CD."

A strange but beautiful ballad wafted through the kitchen. The haunting melody from the flute gave it a Celtic lilt. The lyrics described a secret love and a waning harvest moon.

Sarah gave a sigh. "They don't sound dangerous, except in a sentimental heartbreak way."

"They're amazing," Jeremy said. "It's a stroke of luck that they were available for the wedding. Their home base is Portland."

Maddox rushed into the kitchen from the dining room. In his hand, he carried the computer screen with the camera views. "We have a problem."

The feed from the camera that faced the edge of the cliff to the south showed a camouflaged figure moving through the trees. He appeared to be carrying a rifle.

If it was only one man, Blake figured that he and Jeremy could easily handle the threat. They'd been in the same eight-man ranger squad for two tours in Afghanistan. The tricky part would be to capture the intruder without harming him. Having backup would be useful.

"Are the twins still here?" Blake asked Maddox.

"They left ten minutes ago."

He would have preferred using the twins instead of Maddox, who he hadn't worked with before. "Do you see anybody else on the camera feeds?"

Maddox shook his head. "The intruder appears to be alone."

"Have you had sniper training?"

"I can handle a rifle."

"Weapons and ammo are in the front closet. Position yourself on the porch and monitor the camera feeds. If you see another intruder, call my sat phone."

"What should I do?" Sarah asked.

Once again, they were in the midst of a potentially dangerous situation. This time, he'd keep her on the sidelines. "Stay here. Make sure all doors are locked and don't let people go near the windows."

In the dining room, Blake gave a quick explanation to the people around the breakfast table, which now included the band, while Jeremy stole a dramatic kiss from his fiancée. They armed themselves from the weapons cache in the front closet, and Blake gave the orders. "I'll come in from the north. You take the southern approach. If you have to shoot, don't go for a kill shot. I want to talk to this guy and get information."

As they prepared to leave, Alvardo joined them from his bedroom. He immediately deduced what was happening. "I can help," he said.

"Stay with Maddox."

Blake might have been able to put him to better use, but he didn't want to take the time to explain. The sooner they nabbed the intruder, the better. He and Jeremy exited through the door on the far south end of the hallway and pulled it tight so it locked behind them.

They could have taken one of the screens showing the camera feed to pinpoint the location of the intruder, but Blake had a fairly good idea of where he was. "About a hundred and twenty yards away," he said in low, quiet tones, "near that fork in the path."

"I know the spot," Jeremy said. "There's not much level ground around here, but I think I can get behind him."

Without further discussion of strategy, they adopted a maneuver they'd used many times before—a pincer with the intruder trapped in the middle. Blake doubted they'd be able to use the element of surprise in the daylight. In their jeans and jackets, they weren't invisible amid the trees and boulders. Though both men were trained to move with a minimum of noise, the silence of the forest magnified every sound. It wasn't snowing but the air was ice-cold. A coating of snow from last night covered the ground.

When he had eyes on the intruder, Blake ducked behind a waist-high boulder and watched as the man in gray-and-white camouflage crept timidly toward the house, stopping frequently to look around. His face was covered by a knit gray ski mask. He wore a backpack and carried a semiautomatic rifle.

The forest didn't appear to be his natural habitat. He was breathing heavily, and he stumbled over twigs and pinecones. He didn't hold his weapon like a hunter or a soldier, which caused Blake to wonder what the intruder's plan was. If he wasn't a marksman, why would he attempt a shooting?

Blake moved to a vantage point uphill from the winding path. Through the trees, he saw Jeremy take his position behind a tree trunk.

The intruder was about forty yards from the south end of the house when Blake fired a warning shot and shouted, "Drop your weapon!"

Instead of obeying, the intruder swung his rifle in a half circle, wildly spraying bullets. "Don't shoot at me. I'm warning you. Don't shoot."

Blake recognized the voice. This was the guy he'd talked to on the phone last night—the kidnapper. "You're surrounded," Blake said. "If you don't drop your weapon, we will open fire."

"No, don't shoot." He threw the rifle into the bare branches of a chokecherry bush. "I'm carrying a bomb."

"A bomb."

"That's right, an explosive device or whatever

you military people call it. I was going to plant it at the house."

Blake stepped out from his hiding place so the intruder could see him, but he didn't approach the guy. Keeping his voice calm, he asked, "Is the bomb in your backpack?"

"Don't come any closer." The intruder waved a metallic blue cell phone. "This is how I detonate it. Come any closer, and I'll set it off, I swear I will."

"Come on, man. That's a nasty way to die. You don't want to commit suicide."

"And I don't want to go to prison. Stay away from me and nobody gets hurt."

Last night, Blake had thought the kidnapper was the mastermind who hired Farley and his men. But this frightened man didn't have the attitude or the smarts to be a leader. "Who are you working for? Give me a name. I can cut you a deal."

"Some names are better left unsaid." His voice trembled. He was scared. "Leave me alone."

"Is anyone else with you?"

"It's just me."

His answer came so quickly that Blake believed him. There wasn't a team of assassins. "But you're taking orders from someone else."

The intruder shook his head but didn't verbally deny the accusation. Blake continued, "You're not the kind of man who hires thugs to do kidnappings. You don't know how to build a bomb. You shouldn't have to take the fall for this. If you're being forced or coerced, I can help you."

"I didn't want anyone to be hurt." He sounded like he was on the verge of tears. "I still don't."

"I understand," Blake said. "Take off the backpack, put it on the ground and come with me."

The intruder hesitated for a moment. He seemed to be considering surrender. Then he looked beyond Blake's shoulder and saw something that spooked him.

Blake glanced back. Maddox and Alvardo were approaching with rifles held at the ready. They had picked exactly the wrong time to show up. He gestured for them to stay back as he spoke to the intruder. "They're not going to shoot."

The intruder turned and stumbled. When he looked up, he saw Jeremy blocking the path to his escape.

"Move." The intruder waved his cell phone again. "Get the hell out of my way."

As soon as Jeremy stepped back, the other man bolted. He lurched through the forest, crashing into low-hanging branches and trampling bushes at the edge of the path. Though he seemed to be staying on the pathways, he left a trail that a blind man could follow.

Blake turned to Alvardo and Maddox. "Return to the B and B and keep watch."

"What are you going to do?" Alvardo demanded.

For a military man, he sure as hell didn't understand chain of command. Blake was the ranking officer; he gave the orders. "If I need you, I'll call Maddox on the sat phone."

He pivoted and jogged down the path toward Jeremy.

"I could have tackled him," Jeremy said.

"Not worth the risk. You might have triggered the bomb." Blake looked down the pathway. "Where does this lead?"

"It's the Cascade Path. It goes downhill and then up to a waterfall that Sarah calls the Cascade. I'm not sure that's an official name."

It was a good thing that he'd stopped the intruder. If this guy had managed to set up his explosive and damage the B and B, Sarah would have hunted him down and shown no mercy.

"Can we drive to the waterfall?"

"No."

"The intruder must have used a snowmobile to get there." Because they hadn't heard an engine, it was safe to assume that the snowmobile wasn't nearby. "We can't let him get to his ride. Jeremy, you know this area better than I do. Take the lead."

He ran behind his buddy, scanning the area as they charged down the path, following the footprints the intruder had left in the snow. He spotted the gray-and-white camo and pointed. "Up there."

The highest part of the path narrowed to a rocky

ledge and was covered with snow, which made the footing difficult. If they couldn't catch up to the intruder, they'd have to shoot him in the leg and bring him down. Blake wasn't going to let this guy escape.

Following Jeremy, he powered up the slope. The two rangers were in far better physical condition than the intruder and were closing the distance between them.

Again, Blake tried to reason with the guy. He shouted, "Take off the backpack and step away from it. We can help you."

"He's not listening," Jeremy said.

He was listening, all right, but he was too scared to do what Blake said. The real mastermind—the person who had given the order to plant a bomb—had inspired terror in the intruder.

At the highest point in the path, they were only twenty yards away from the man with the backpack. He stood on a path that went behind the waterfall. Though mostly frozen in jagged spears, water still dripped along the edges and inside the ice, creating an illusion of movement as it descended fifty feet to a rocky pool.

The intruder peeled off his backpack and laid it on the ground. He held up his cell phone. "All it takes to detonate the explosion is for me to hit this button. If I were you, I'd take cover."

The intruder darted into the cavelike area behind the waterfall. He was hidden by shadow. And they couldn't risk moving closer. The bomb made a damn effective roadblock.

"He's getting away," Blake said. He couldn't believe this guy had outsmarted him. Jeremy had already moved farther back on the trail. "I'm not getting any closer to that backpack."

"What's on the other side of the overhang?"

"I've never gone that far."

Blake descended the path they'd just climbed. He hoped he could find an angle where he could see the intruder well enough to get a shot at him.

A frantic scream pierced the air.

Leaning over the edge of the path, Blake saw the man in gray-and-white camouflage as he tumbled, clawing at rocks and snow, tearing a gash in the steep cliff. He couldn't break his fall. Momentum carried him the last several feet into the frozen pool at the bottom of the waterfall.

The man wasn't dead. Sobbing incoherently, he struggled to stand. His bare hands were slick with blood. He'd lost his ski mask and was bleeding from a wound near his temple. The dark red contrasted the white and gray of the rocks and forest. When he attempted to stand, his right leg collapsed under his weight. He sprawled facedown at the edge of the pond.

It was going to take a mountain rescue to get

him safely up the cliff. First, Blake needed to deal with the bomb.

"He's not going anywhere," Jeremy said, "but he's still trying to move."

"Does he have the phone?"

"I can't tell."

"Let's hope not."

Blake covered the distance between them and the backpack in seconds. He picked up the satchel by a strap and flung it as hard as he could into the forest.

Both he and Jeremy ducked.

They didn't hear an explosion.

Chapter Eleven

When Sarah got the emergency call from Blake, she responded as quickly as possible. In a storage cabinet in the mudroom, she had the ropes, carabiners, belaying equipment and climbing gear needed for a mountain rescue. It was too much to carry by herself so she called out, "Emily, I need your help."

"I thought you'd never ask."

Sarah gave her a dubious look. "You don't like rock climbing, and you hate the sight of blood. How come you're such an eager beaver?"

"Jeremy," she said simply.

Sarah nodded. "Put together a pack with climbing gear."

Sarah organized her own pack with first aid supplies and a couple of thermal Mylar blankets.

"First aid," Emily noted. "Who's hurt?"

"Blake said the guy they were chasing took a fall. I'm trying to be prepared."

Alvardo and Maddox stood in the doorway

that led to the kitchen. Alvardo said, "We're coming, too."

"Not this time," she said. "Blake wanted help with a rescue that requires climbing. Emily and I know this area."

"Excuse me, Sarah, but I don't take orders from you."

Alvardo sounded as whiny as a kid on a playground. Her standard speech about how she was in charge of whatever happened in her B and B probably wasn't going to change his childish attitude. "Call Blake on the sat phone. If he gives the okay, I'm fine with it."

In less than five minutes, she and Emily were geared up and ready to roll. They strode through the kitchen to the front door. Alvardo sat at the dining room table, pouting. Maddox was on the front porch, keeping watch. He waved as the two women rushed into the forest toward the Cascade Path where Blake and Jeremy were waiting.

A combination of adrenaline and relief pumped through her bloodstream. When Sarah had first heard gunfire outside the B and B, she'd imagined the worst. Luckily, the place where Blake and the man in camouflage had their confrontation was within the scope of one of the camera feeds. She could see that he was unharmed. Her fears subsided.

Then Maddox and Alvardo had returned to the

B and B and started talking about an explosive device. Her misgivings had taken on a sharper edge, slicing away at her self-control. In the silence that followed while Blake and Jeremy were out of camera range and pursuing the intruder, she'd almost lost it. She felt dizzy. If anyone had spoken to her, she wouldn't have been able to answer. It had taken a conscious effort to regain her control…and that worried her.

Sarah wasn't the sort of woman who flew into a panic. Her trademark was holding things together and not getting scared. But the possibility of something bad happening to Blake was terrifying. She barely knew the man. And yet, he was vastly important to her. If he came to harm, she'd be devastated and would probably spend the rest of her life playing sad ballads from Ollie and the Dewdrops about lost loves and lost lovers.

As she and Emily jogged the last few yards to the place where their two army rangers were standing, she envied her friend's unbridled, passionate reaction to seeing her fiancé. Emily threw her arms around Jeremy and kissed him hard.

Sarah didn't have the right to embrace Blake. They weren't in a relationship. But when she looked at him, her heart soared. She was overjoyed to find him safe.

He lightly touched her arm. "Thanks for—"

"Don't ever do that again," she snapped, covering her emotion with irritation. "You scared me half to death."

He wasn't put off by her gruff manner. Instead, he grinned. "You were worried about me."

"If you injured yourself on my property, it would have driven my insurance premiums through the roof."

"You care about me."

He was teasing, again. And she wouldn't give him the satisfaction of showing him how much she cared. "What's this about a bomb?"

"The intruder said he was carrying an explosive device in his backpack."

"Was he?"

Blake shrugged. "I don't know. I threw the backpack out of the way and it didn't explode."

"What was he planning to do with a bomb?" As soon as she spoke, the answer was obvious. "He was going to blow up the B and B."

"That was his plan."

"That bastard!" The threat to her home upset her but not as much as the idea of Blake being in mortal danger. "Then what happened?"

"He tried to run, went through the passageway behind the waterfall. He must have lost his footing. The next thing we knew, he'd fallen."

From the edge of the path, he pointed down to where the body of a man wearing gray-and-white camouflage sprawled on the rocks at the foot of the waterfall. Red splotches of blood stood out on his clothes. His eyes were squeezed shut. She could see him trembling and knew enough about mountain rescue to recognize the symptoms of trauma.

"He's going into shock," she said. "He needs treatment."

"I put in a call to Kovak. He and the mountain rescue unit will be here as soon as possible."

"Good," she said. "We'll need them to handle the evacuation. I've got ropes and carabiners, but I don't have professional rescue equipment, like an emergency carry litter or a spine board to immobilize the victim."

"Kovak said you'd had experience with rescues."

"I've taken some classes but I'm not fully trained." She stared down at the man who had intended to blow up her house. Even though he was the scum of the earth, she couldn't deny him aid. "We should get down to him and start treatment."

"You know the area. Where's the best place to set the ropes?"

"If we go through the passage behind the waterfall, there's an easy descent on the other side. All hiking, no climbing."

"How long does it take?"

"Only a few minutes more than belaying."

She sorted items into one of the large hiking backpacks, including a thermal blanket, water bottles and her first aid kit. As she prepared to hoist it onto her back, Blake caught the shoulder strap.

"Let me carry it," he said.

She held the strap. "I can manage."

"I'm sure you can. I'm just trying to be useful."

There was no point in getting into a tug-of-war. She let go of the pack and watched as he adjusted the straps for his wide shoulders.

Emily eased up beside her and whispered, "Sometimes, it's nice to let somebody else carry the load."

The symbolism wasn't wasted on Sarah. "I'm not used to having help."

"Accept it and smile," Emily advised. "There's nothing wrong with being treated like a lady."

"As long as he knows who's boss." She stepped back and started issuing orders. "You and Jeremy stay here and wait for Kovak. Blake, follow me."

The space behind the waterfall was a miniature cave that was open across the front. The path was about twenty feet long, and the ceiling was only six feet tall at the highest point. Blake had to duck to avoid hitting his head. With the additional bulk of the backpack, he barely fit inside. He didn't complain.

And she didn't point out that it would have been easier for her to carry the pack. Emily was right. Sarah didn't have to do everything by herself.

Inside the cave, the air was cool, quiet and mysterious. She'd always loved this secret hideaway. In the warm days of summer, rainbows danced in the glittering water. In winter, the falls formed a jagged, icy curtain.

She picked her way carefully across the frozen granite floor. "Watch your step."

"It's beautiful in here."

She turned to face him. Though it was urgent for them to reach the injured man, she wanted to make a memory of her and Blake in a place that was special to her. An odd blue-tinted light filtered through the ice and shone on his high cheekbones and sharp jawline. She blinked, taking a mental snapshot of this moment. Softly, she confided, "I used to come here when I was a kid and hide from the rest of the world."

"When you got in trouble with your parents," he said.

"That wasn't the reason. I don't run away from trouble. If I've done something wrong, I'll stand up and take my punishment."

"Why did you need to hide?"

Talking about herself wasn't Sarah's favorite thing. She'd never gone to a therapist, and she kept a distance between herself and most other people. Sharing made her vulnerable. "There isn't time right now for me to explain."

His blue-eyed gaze locked with hers. "You can tell me anything, Sarah."

"Maybe I will, but not right now."

She emerged on the other side. The path clung to the side of the steep, rocky cliff. A few yards away, they could see the place where the intruder had stumbled over a protruding, slanted rock at the edge.

"Looks like he plummeted straight down," she said. "That scraggly pine tree broke his fall, but he didn't stop there. He bounced off the rocks the rest of the way down."

"There was blood on his head," he said, "but he was conscious when he hit the bottom."

"He could still have a concussion," she said. "We need to hurry."

Moving quickly but cautiously, she followed the narrow path on the cliff around a fat, jutting boulder. Someday, she hoped to improve this path enough for her guests to explore this area. For now, she kept it blocked off with warning signs.

On the other side of the boulder, the path widened and the descent was more gradual. A thicket of pine trees marked the beginning of the forest. She stepped off the path and went into the trees, clinging to branches to keep from slipping. Though the waterfall was to the west, she went in the opposite direction where the land was more level.

At the edge of a four-foot drop, Blake joined her. "How much farther?"

"There's the creek." She pointed. "We follow that, and we'll be at the waterfall in a couple of minutes."

"Is there a place around here where he could have parked a snowmobile?"

"Anywhere," she said. "The snow is kind of light under the trees in the forest, but you don't need tons of snow to use one of those nasty things."

"Not a fan of snowmobiling?"

"They're too loud. They scare the animals. And they tear up the landscape." She paused. "But it's kind of fun to ride really fast."

They slipped over the drop and covered the ground quickly, walking side by side near the creek. Blake didn't seem to have any difficulty keeping up with her pace. "The elevation doesn't bother you," she said.

"I'm acclimated," he said. "Much of Afghanistan is mountains."

The terrain in that foreign land on the other side of the globe hadn't occurred to her. She'd never left the United States, hadn't spent much time away from her native Colorado. Afghanistan sounded unbelievably exotic. His life was very different from hers. "Are you going to miss the travel after you retire?"

"I can still travel," he said, "and the best part is being able to visit places I want to see. The army didn't give me a choice."

"Where do you want to go?"

"Australia," he said without hesitation. "I've never been there."

"I'd like to go to Naples and see the ruins at Mount Vesuvius." She'd read a book about the eruption of the ancient volcano and the excavation at Pompeii. "After that, I'd tour the Mediterranean, especially the Greek islands."

"Have you done much traveling?"

"It's hard to get away from the B and B."

But she had always dreamed about faraway lands. When she was a kid hiding inside her cave behind the waterfall, she fantasized about opening her eyes and seeing a whole different world. And she would be different, too. No more practical, down-to-earth Sarah. She would be sophisticated and smart, like an artist in Paris or an archaeologist in the tombs of ancient Egypt or an explorer on the Amazon. Childish dreams, she'd never shared them with anyone.

As they came around the last curve in the creek, she saw the fallen man in gray-and-white camouflage fatigues and hurried toward him. He lay on his side with his arms pulled up against his chest. His right foot twisted at an impossible angle, probably due to a broken ankle. The red smears of blood from a head wound contrasted his ashen complexion. His lips were blue.

Before she reached him, Blake stopped her. “Let me do a body check for hidden weapons.”

He shrugged off the backpack on the rocks beside the barely conscious man and knelt beside him. In a thorough pat-down, Blake found the man’s wallet and a hunting knife in a belt sheath. Not that the injured man appeared to be capable of attacking them.

She glanced toward the place where he’d fallen and saw a flash of metallic blue. Crossing the rocks, she picked up a cell phone and held it so Blake could see. “Do you think this is his?”

“Be careful with that.” His tone was sharp. “Don’t press any numbers.”

“What’s the big deal?”

“That’s the detonator for the bomb.”

Not what she wanted to hear. Handling the metallic phone as carefully as an egg with a cracked shell, she tiptoed across the rocks toward him. “Most of a phone number is already on the screen.”

“If the last numbers are punched, I expect the bomb to blow.”

“Where is it?”

“I’m not sure.” Standing, he took the phone from her, turned off the power and stashed it in the pocket of his leather bomber jacket. He was casual as though he handled bombs on a regular basis, which he probably did.

But she didn’t. A shudder went through her. She

tried to tell herself there was nothing to fear. Even if the bomb exploded, the fire wouldn't spread in this damp air. Controlled explosive charges were common in the mountains. The ski patrols used them to control avalanche danger and to clear landslides.

"Do you think the bomb is nearby?"

"I threw the pack from the high point on the path. It's probably over that way." He pointed over his shoulder. "Are you going to help me with this guy or what?"

"Of course, I am."

Being with Blake had triggered her imagination, and she couldn't afford the luxury of dreaming. She needed practical focus. In the backpack, she found a thermal blanket that was a little more heavy-duty than most of those thin Mylar sheets. Keeping him warm was the first step in treating shock. When she tucked the silver blanket around him, he winced and moaned.

"I'd like to get the blanket under him," she said, "but I don't think we should move him."

Blake squatted on the opposite side of the injured man. He opened the black leather wallet and flipped to the ID. "The driver's license says his name is Norman Franks, and he's from Denver."

She took a water bottle from her backpack and twisted off the cap. "Norman," she said loudly. "Norman, I want you to take a drink."

His eyelids pinched but there was no other reaction to his name. His breathing was quick and shallow. Knowing that dehydration was an issue, she held the bottle to his mouth and tilted his head so he wouldn't choke. He barely managed a sip.

Blake leaned over him. "Too bad you can't talk to me, Norman. I've got questions."

"You'll have to wait," she said.

Blake didn't give up. "Norman, who are you working for? Give me a name."

"Stop it. He can't talk."

"I guess not." Blake moved down the body to inspect Norman's ankle. "There's a lot of swelling. I should get his shoe off."

"There are supplies in my pack for splinting."

"I'll see what I can do."

It made sense that Blake would know how to handle emergency procedures; he was a soldier who had gone to the aid of those injured in battle. While she cleaned the head wound, he used bandages and an inflatable splint to immobilize the injured ankle so Norman could be transported when the rescue team got here.

After she bandaged the bloody gash on his forehead, she made another attempt with the water bottle.

Norman grabbed her arm. His eyes flashed open. His mouth gaped. He was trying to speak.

"What is it?" she asked. "What do you want to tell me?"

Blake was close beside her. "Talk to us, Norman."

His fingers were like claws digging through her parka. His body convulsed. He shivered from head to toe. Then his eyes slammed shut and he released his grasp.

He lay very still, barely breathing.

Chapter Twelve

If there had been a way to keep score, Blake would have said that his team was winning. Kovak and the mountain rescue team had evacuated Norman Franks, aka the kidnapper, aka the intruder, to the hospital in Aspen. His injuries had been treated. He was under guard and still unresponsive. There was no indication that he had been working with an active partner. The arrest status of his dupes, Farley and his friends, hadn't changed. And there hadn't been any other threats.

On the minus side, a search team from the sheriff's department failed to find the bomb. Their theory was that when Blake threw it, the pack had gotten hung up in high tree branches. When the weather cleared, they'd come back with a chopper to search from overhead.

At two o'clock in the afternoon, a light snow was beginning to dribble down from cloudy skies. The forecast for tomorrow was eight to twelve inches. The morning after that was the wedding ceremony, and then he'd be leaving on Sunday. Not sure how he felt about that.

Blake stood on the landing at the top of the staircase in the B and B and rested his elbows on the rail as he looked down at the front entrance. Senator Hank Layton and his wife, Rebecca, were expected to arrive at any minute.

He quietly watched as Sarah steamed across the entryway and caught up to Alvardo, who was on his way out of the front room. She waved her mobile phone, connected with the landline, at him. Her angry voice carried.

"I've got a bone to pick, Alvardo."

He slowly turned to face her. His jaw was tight. His earlier appreciation of her charms was no longer evident. "What's your problem?"

"You called the florist and told them they weren't allowed to enter. *Really?* Do you *really* think that somebody who works for a shop named Roses and Ribbons is dangerous?"

"I ran a background check," Alvardo said. "Two employees have criminal records. They were arrested for causing a public disturbance four years ago."

"So what?" Sarah planted one fist on her hip and gestured with the phone. Though Blake couldn't see her face, he knew she'd be glaring, shooting lightning bolts from her dark eyes. "Emily has a worse criminal record than that, and she's the most innocent person I've ever known."

"I'm doing as I was ordered. Nobody with a record gets access to the house."

"Then, you're going to meet the florist's truck at the kitchen door and unload all the flowers yourself. I'll inform you when they arrive."

She turned on her heel and stalked down the hall toward the kitchen. Alvardo cursed under his breath at her retreating form.

Blake almost laughed out loud. As far as he was concerned, Alvardo had gotten the dressing-down that he deserved because he hadn't followed orders precisely. Blake had said to inform him before taking action, and he would have given a pass to the Roses and Ribbons crew. Alvardo's obsessive-compulsive behavior was annoying. Still, it was better for him to be too careful instead of too lax.

The honking of a car horn from the front brought Emily running from the kitchen. She unlocked the front door and dashed onto the porch. Her shouts of delight rang through the house as she dragged a tall, thin man with graying hair inside and hugged her mother—a slender, graceful woman in a white ski jacket with a fake fur collar. When Jeremy joined them, there were hugs and kisses all around. Everybody talked. Everybody laughed.

The touchy-feely reunion of the Layton family contrasted the air of formality when the general had made his entrance. If it was true that opposites attracted, these two families would be bonded in no time. Blake doubted that would happen.

He noticed Sarah standing at the edge of the excitement. She wore her professional, innkeeper smile, welcoming her guests and assuring them that they'd be well cared for. She was good at masking her deeper emotions under a layer of efficiency and practicality, but he'd seen a different side to her. In the cave behind the waterfall, she had relaxed her guard. Last night when they'd kissed, he had felt her passion.

She glanced up and saw him on the landing. Her lips curved in a smile that seemed to be meant only for him. He might have been reading too much into her expression, but he imagined that she was thinking of their kiss. Holding her gaze, he came down the staircase and was immediately engulfed in a whirlpool of Layton family goodwill with introductions and hugs, even from the senator. Sarah had also been sucked into the happy vortex.

A young blond man with puppy-dog eyes came through the open door, carrying two large suitcases. "Hate to interrupt," he said, "but there are six more of these to unload."

"Eight suitcases?" Emily rolled her eyes. "Mom, you're only going to be here for three days."

"Half of it is yours," Rebecca Layton said. "I

have your bridal gown. And a perfect dress for you, Sarah. And I brought supplies for a spa day tomorrow."

Under her breath, Sarah said, "Please don't tell me you packed your own masseuse."

"Lotions, potions and oils," Rebecca said. "We're going to smell like a garden."

Blake introduced himself to the blond man—the senator's speechwriter, whose name was Horatio Harrison Waverly-Smythe III. He asked to be called Skip.

Blake waved him toward the door. "Come on, Skip. Let's get that van unloaded."

"Their rooms are upstairs in the left wing," Sarah said. "I'll show you when you come back in."

"Where's Jeremy's father?" the senator asked. "I've been looking forward to meeting him."

The happy merry-go-round stalled. The senator versus general confrontation wasn't anybody's idea of a good time. In the back of their collective minds, they'd all been dreading it. The time was almost here.

Emily giggled and laced her arm through her father's. "Daddy, I want you to come upstairs with me first. Let me show you around. You've never been here."

Her mother backed her up. "That's right, Hank. You weren't able to come with me when I visited

Bentley's B and B. You're going to love the history. Teddy Roosevelt slept here. Isn't he one of your favorite presidents?"

"I like Teddy."

"Lots of celebrities have stayed here," Emily said. "Sarah has a wall of photos in her office. Clark Gable and Marlene Deitrich and Gregory Peck."

"Oh, I'd like to see those pictures."

"First, we go upstairs," Rebecca said. "Let's unpack."

The senator allowed himself to be dragged up the staircase.

Crisis averted.

Outside in the light snow, Blake hoisted a trunk-size suitcase from the airport van and glanced at Jeremy. "What do you think is going to happen when they meet?"

"They're civilized men," Jeremy said tentatively. "They have their differences, but they won't lose control. They'll probably just stare at each other in icy silence."

"You think?" Blake went up the steps to the porch. "I'm betting on a slap fight."

"I'll take that bet," Skip said as he met them at the door. "Senator Layton has been working out. Fifty bucks says they never get past the handshake that turns into a test of who can squeeze harder."

Inside the house, Sarah heard just enough to

guess what was going on. In a whisper, she said, "I can't believe it. Are you betting on what happens when they meet?"

Blake nodded. "What do you think—icy silence, slap fight or aggressive handshake?"

"None of the above," she said. "The general has been drinking since lunch. He's going to throw his single malt whiskey in the senator's face."

"No way," Jeremy said. "Not my dad. Throwing drinks is too girlie, and he never wastes his single malt."

Skip was keeping score. "Care to make it interesting, Sarah? Fifty bucks?"

"Why not?" She shot them all a stern gaze. "Don't say anything about this to Emily."

Upstairs, they went to the bedrooms on the left. Sarah had thought far enough ahead to house the general and his aides in the right wing on the opposite end of the house. The last bedroom on that side would be occupied by the twins, who were moving in later today to provide full-time security until after the wedding.

When they unloaded and shuffled things around, it became apparent that the Laytons' luggage would require its own room.

"We're going to need a full-length mirror in here," Rebecca said. "And a freestanding rack to hang the gowns."

"I'll take care of it," Emily said.

"Don't worry," Sarah reassured her. "Blake can help me move things around."

He nodded agreement. Until now, his primary concern had been security for the B and B. He hadn't realized how much effort had gone into the wedding preparations. He'd gotten off easy. His only duty as best man was planning the bachelor party, and he'd delegated the finding of a stripper to Alvardo. Maybe he ought to check with Sarah about beer and snack food.

"The B and B is almost full," she said to him. "If the snow gets bad and the women I have helping with the cooking and housekeeping have to stay, I've got one vacant room downstairs and one at the end of this hall."

"Plus the dormitory space in the attic where the band is staying." He stood beside her and watched as Emily and her mother tried to divert the senator with unpacking duties. "And you've got that big bedroom in the downstairs south wing."

"That's the nicest suite in the house," she said. "I'm keeping it open, just in case."

"In case of what?"

"If we get hit by a blizzard, the airport will close down and the newlyweds will have to stay here after the ceremony."

"And the big bedroom becomes the honeymoon suite."

She nodded. "Not as good as their planned trip to Jamaica. At least, they'll have some privacy."

The senator had changed from his parka to an argyle sweater vest worn over a dark brown turtleneck and jeans. He straightened his narrow shoulders and hitched up his belt. "I'd like to meet General Hamilton now. Jeremy, does your father go by Charlie or Chuck?"

"You'll have to ask him, sir."

Blake suppressed a chuckle. If the liberal senator marched up to the general and called him Chuck, the odds were good for a slap fight.

With the senator and Jeremy leading the way, they filed down the staircase and went into the front room. The general sat in the heavy leather chair beside the fireplace. Alvardo was opposite him. Maddox was nowhere in sight, and Blake assumed he'd taken a position in the office where he could monitor all the camera feeds.

The general rose to his feet. He wasn't a particularly large man, but he was solid as a brick wall. His neatly trimmed white hair caught the light from the fire. His nondescript expression reminded Blake of a man facing a potential foe, ready to smile or to snarl.

The senator approached with hand outstretched. "I'm Henry Layton. Call me Hank."

The general darted a glance at Sarah, perhaps

recalling their first meeting when she teased about his name. Calmly, he said, "I'm Charles."

When they shook hands, the air in the room felt electrified. Blake wouldn't have been surprised to see sparks flaring between them, but the handshake ended without incident. Hank introduced Rebecca and his speechwriter, Skip. The general did the same with Alvardo.

Then it was quiet—the icy silence Jeremy had predicted.

Emily tried to start a nonconfrontational conversation. "Jeremy and I thought we could have the ceremony in this room. The justice of the peace can stand right over here, and I can come down the staircase."

Hank hadn't moved away from the general. He stood a few inches taller. His graying hair was longer and fell across his forehead. There was something of the trustworthy small-town lawyer about him, and Blake remembered Jeremy telling him that Hank Layton liked to think of himself as a modern-day Atticus Finch. Though his argyle sweater vest was more casual than Charles's tweed jacket, the senator held himself with an air of authority. After all, he was a senator, and it took a high degree of determination to reach that political station.

Likewise, the general was a leader, accustomed to having men jump to do his bidding. They faced off like a couple of old lions. Not growling at each other, but wary.

Hank spoke first. "I want you to know that I don't blame you for the attempted kidnapping, Charles. In fact, I'm not sure that the perpetrator wasn't coming after me."

The general lifted his chin. "You have enemies. I'm aware of that."

"Some are violent," Hank said. "I'm not accusing anyone, but I've angered some groups that are armed and dangerous. You see, I'm pro–gun control."

"Of course you are."

Blake could see the gloves coming off. His bet on a slap fight was looking more likely.

"I'd like to suggest," Hank said, "for the duration of the weekend, that we follow the example of Emily and Jeremy. We can agree to disagree, without discussion or rancor."

"You're quite a little mediator," Charles said.

"That's my job."

"Glad you told me. I've often wondered what you people do in the Senate."

"As opposed to what you do in the Pentagon." Hank's gray eyes turned to flint. "That's pretty damned clear, isn't it?"

"Protecting human rights," the general said, "making the world safe for democracy. That's what I do."

"Agree to disagree."

Emily attempted to insert herself between them. "Okay, you two. That's enough."

The general squared off. "If you senators took the time to understand what we do at the Pentagon, you wouldn't be so quick to chop our funding."

"If you learned to spend responsibly, we wouldn't have to treat you like spoiled children."

"Unbelievable. You're lecturing me about responsibility when you can't even pass a budget."

"Stop it," Emily said.

"Take off the blinders, Charles. The army works for the people of this country, and that's who I represent."

"Don't do this." Emily stamped her foot.

"Honey," her father said, "I'm being more than fair."

"For a change," Charles said.

"Don't interrupt when I'm speaking to my daughter."

"Stop." Emily grabbed the general's drink from the table and threw it at her father. "Listen to me."

Charles smirked. "You heard the little lady."

She swung around and punched his arm hard enough that the general involuntarily winced.

"I'm talking to both of you," Emily said. "This is my wedding, and I'm not going to put up with this behavior. We're family. Whether you like it or not, we're all going to get along."

Blake watched in amazement. A drink in the face. And a slap fight. Both delivered by Emily. He hadn't seen this coming.

Chapter Thirteen

Other than gagging the two men and locking them in rooms on opposite ends of the B and B, Sarah didn't know how she could keep them from arguing. She hoped the combined goodwill from everyone else would keep a lid on this simmering volcano, but it was hard to entrust that job to others. This was her inn, her responsibility. *I can't control everything.* The trick was to find a way to calm down and maintain her equilibrium.

When the Roses and Ribbons truck arrived, she enforced her threat to Alvardo to make him do the unloading. Emily and her mother told him where to place the various centerpieces of white and red roses combined with calla lilies and bright green foliage. Though the roses were supposed to be a variety that didn't smell too much, the fragrance was overwhelming. She told them to store the arching display that would be used in the ceremony in the honeymoon suite with the door closed.

After fielding a call from the caterer, who was

nervous about the snow, she agreed with him that he and his two-man crew should plan to stay after they arrived. That meant three more people for Friday night and Saturday. Then she checked on the progress of dinner with the two women she'd hired to help out. There were a dozen more tasks that needed to be done. It was time to start delegating.

Sarah tapped Blake on the shoulder. "Grab your gloves and jacket and meet me at the kitchen door. I need some help."

"You got it, lady."

In the mudroom, she zipped up her parka and unlocked the door. Outside the gently falling snow brushed her cheeks. The cold refreshed her. She inhaled a deep, moist breath. "How about that Emily," he said. "I didn't think she had the guts to stand up to her dad and the general."

"She might look like a cupcake, but she's not all sweetness and fluff." Otherwise, their friendship never would have lasted. "Emily is one of those people who can't bear to see injustice. When she's standing up for the underdog, she can take on the world."

"Like you?"

"In a way." Sarah hadn't thought of that similarity. "It's odd. We're kind of alike, but I tend to think of me and Emily as being very different."

"How so?"

"For one thing, she's the world's biggest optimist, and I tend to see the glass as half-empty."

"You're analytical," he said.

"And cynical."

"You look ahead and see the problems before they occur. That's a positive trait."

"Which is much nicer than saying that I'm a big grump."

A covered breezeway spanned the area between the kitchen and a triple-wide garage. An inch of snow had already accumulated on the concrete. She pulled on her gloves, opened the lid on a storage box under the eaves and dug into a bag of eco-friendly deicer, which she scattered across the area.

Blake did the same. "What is this stuff?"

"Deicer made of dried corn and the organic clay product that goes into kitty litter. Not great for the environment but less damaging than rock salt. This back door is where all the supplies for the wedding are going to be delivered, and I don't want anybody to slip and fall."

He followed her example, going all the way to the driveway. "What other ways are you and Emily different?"

"She comes from a privileged background, and my family is frugal. Some might say the Bentleys are cheap."

"Owning one of the classiest bed-and-breakfasts in the Aspen area isn't a poor man's occupation."

"That shows how much you know." She scattered the deicer near the garage door. "When the economy started to fail, the hospitality industry took a big hit. People were afraid to spend their hard-earned dollars on vacations. All the hotels were suffering. I've been lucky."

"How so?"

"The B and B isn't a big operation, and I don't have much overhead. Even so, I've had to cut back. Carrie—the woman who I called to help out in the kitchen—used to be full-time. Now I only contact her when I need extra help."

"Didn't you have Emily working for you one summer?"

"Yes, but she didn't take a full salary. She was more of an intern and a great help." They'd been like sisters, rising together and working together. After college, Emily had needed to put distance between herself and her high-powered parents. And Sarah had needed a friend to make the transition from being part of a family to the sole proprietor of the B and B. "That was a couple of months before she met Jeremy."

"They're good together."

Dusting off his gloves, he moved closer to her. His nearness reminded her of feelings she'd put aside. Her attraction to him was palpable, a magnetic force, and she didn't want to give in to it.

Not yet, anyway. She stepped away from him. "I brought you out here because I have a job for you."

"Okay."

"I'm putting you in charge of the fire." *Baby, won't you light my fire.*

"No problem," he said. "What other ways are you and Emily different?"

She avoided looking up at him, fearful of letting her guard down. "You're like a dog with a bone. Don't you ever give up?"

"Never." His deep, rich voice struck just the right chord inside her. "You don't talk much about yourself, and I want to follow this thread to the end."

"Here's the big difference," she said. "Emily is beautiful, stunningly beautiful."

"And so are you."

"Don't get me wrong, I don't have low self-esteem, and I know I'm not bad-looking. But Emily is special. She's the sort of woman who can stop traffic."

In short, she was a princess.

"And that's what you want to be."

"Maybe," she admitted.

Sarah would never trade her self-sufficient, strong personality for a tiara, but she wouldn't mind being pampered, praised and adored for a little while. Didn't every woman want to be cherished above all others? If Emily got to be gutsy, it was only fair for Sarah to have a moment when she was Cinderella at the ball.

In the meantime, there was firewood to be managed. She grasped the knob on the garage door. Before she could turn it, Blake stopped her.

"Do you keep the garage locked?" he asked.

"No. Why?"

"Anyone has access. This is the first time I've noticed poor security at the B and B." He drew his handgun and stepped in front of her. "What's in there?"

"My truck and an SUV that Emily's been driving are parked at the far end." She let him take the lead. It had never occurred to her that someone might be hiding in here. "When you walk in the door, there's a tool bench in the front and firewood in the back."

"It looks bigger than a regular garage."

"There's an extra space on this side for storage." The garage didn't seem dangerous, except for the saws, the chisels, the screwdrivers and the axes she used for splitting logs. *Axes? Why hadn't she thought of this?* "I've been in and out of here a half dozen times over the past couple of days."

"And you didn't notice anything out of the ordinary."

"Not really." She'd been preoccupied. There had been so much happening with the wedding preparations and the kidnap attempt that she might have strolled past a dancing hippo without paying attention. "I wasn't looking for anything."

"I am."

He yanked open the door and charged into the dark interior. She followed and hit the light switch beside the door. The extra-large garage served the same purpose as a barn on a ranch, creating a space to store the equipment needed in a remote location. Though it wasn't heated, the garage was sealed tightly against the snow and had only a few high windows to let in the light.

She watched as Blake expertly searched the large space, checking under and inside the vehicles and poking into every corner. With his long-legged stride, he covered the area quickly, and he didn't waste a single motion. Returning to her, he tucked his gun into the holster on his hip.

"I had a call from Kovak," he said. "Franks isn't awake yet, but he's not in a coma. We might get information from him. If he doesn't talk, Kovak is working with a cop in Denver to get some background on our kidnapper."

"Do they know anything? Like if he's married or lives with someone?"

"Nothing yet."

"Will you keep me posted?" she asked. "I know there's nothing I can do, but I want to be aware."

He gave a nod. "Kovak also said that they never located the backpack with the bomb."

That threat came much closer to home. "Is it dangerous?"

"Any unexploded device is dangerous." His blue eyes darkened, and his expression was serious. "Franks said the bomb could be detonated using a cell phone."

She remembered the phone number on the screen. "How does that work?"

"The bomb is hooked up to another cell phone inside the device. When the number is called, it's like lighting a fuse."

"But it can't accidentally just go off, right?"

"It depends."

He'd been in the rangers for years. He had seen and experienced a war she couldn't imagine, and he knew firsthand what it meant when a bomb or an IED exploded. Her heart went out to him. Though she could never fully understand what he'd gone through, she respected his courage.

"Firewood," she said, bringing her focus back to the present. "As you can see, I have plenty of split wood stacked inside the garage. It's going to be your job to keep the fire in the front room going. That means taking wood from here and bringing it to the box in the mudroom. From there, you take it to the fireplace."

"Why bother with the middle step of dropping it off in the mudroom?"

"If we have a real blizzard, you won't want to

go outside. Not even to make that little hop from the kitchen door to the garage." She picked up a chunk of wood. "Hold out your arms."

Loaded up with as much split wood as possible, she led him back into the mudroom and opened the lid on the large, half-empty bin. "This should be plenty for today and tomorrow."

After being out in the snow, the warmth of the house wrapped around them like a big, cozy comforter. The aroma of beef stew was a tantalizing reminder that dinner was only an hour and a half away.

"I noticed that you have a snowblower," he said.

"And I should get busy with it," she said. "There's not much daylight left."

"A suggestion," he said. "Let's put the senator in charge of snow removal."

She didn't like the idea. Recruiting guests went against her practices as an innkeeper, even though she hadn't hesitated to give Blake the fireplace responsibility. "I don't think so."

"He's a guy," Blake said. "All guys—even senators—like to play with cool equipment. He's from California. When does he get to use a snowblower?"

"It'd be nice if I didn't have to worry about the snow piling up," she admitted.

"Here's the best part," Blake said with a grin.

"The physical activity might make him too tired to argue."

"You're very persuasive."

"So I've been told." He leaned close enough to give her a kiss on the cheek but didn't. "I'll get him started."

"I have one more thing I need your help with."

She led him up the staircase to the second floor and then onward and upward to the third-floor dormitory where the band was staying. If the blizzard tomorrow made the roads impassable, she'd put the caterer and his staff up here, too. Before reaching the top of the stairs, she called out, "Is everybody decent?"

"Not for years," came the reply. "But come on up."

The guitar player sat cross-legged on a chair by the dormer window. Guitar in hand, he lightly strummed. The other two sprawled on their bellies on the beds. They all made welcoming noises.

"I need to get into storage," she said.

"Can we help?"

"Thanks, but I think this is a one-man job."

She unfastened the combination lock and opened a door that was almost unnoticeable in the pine-paneled wall. Under the eaves were several boxes, taped and neatly labeled. Some were Christmas ornaments. Others held lights, bedding, books and miscellaneous stuff. A full-length mirror leaned horizontally against the inner wall. Not a lovely piece of furniture, it was only a mirror in a simple wood frame with a brace against the back that made it freestanding. It should suit Rebecca's needs.

The mirror was heavier than she'd thought and more unwieldy, but she and Blake managed to get it downstairs. She knocked on the door to the wardrobe bedroom.

Emily's mother answered right away. Her husband stood at the window, staring out at the snow with his hands clasped behind his back.

Sarah had the feeling that she might have interrupted an intense conversation. "I brought the mirror."

"Wonderful," Rebecca said with a bit too much enthusiasm. "I know it isn't really necessary. There's a mirror on the bathroom door, after all. But I wanted Emily to have a chance to see how lovely she is in her gown."

"I'm anxious to see it," Sarah said.

"And your dress, too. I hope it fits. There really isn't time for alterations."

Sarah had recently discovered a distant cousin who was an excellent seamstress, but she lived too far away to make the trek to the B and B with the blizzard coming. "I'm sure it'll be fine."

Rebecca unzipped a garment bag that was lying on the bed and took out a floor-length gown in emerald-green satin. The design and fabric were more formal than anything Sarah had ever worn in her life. She swallowed hard. "I'm not sure I can pull this off."

"Of course you can. You'll be stunning."

Hank Layton turned away from the window and came toward her. "Sarah, I hope you know how much we appreciate all that you're doing for us. These threats are…unfortunate."

"The situation is under control," Blake said. "The sheriff's department has the kidnapper in custody."

"Any clue about his motive?"

"He's still unconscious," Blake said.

"I meant what I said earlier." The tone of his voice was warm and somehow conveyed a note of sincerity that was a plus for a politician. "This could be my fault. I've gotten a number of threats."

"Yes, dear," his wife said. "I'm sure you have just as many enemies as the general."

"Dangerous individuals," Hank said, "the haters and the doubters, the survivalists and the anti-environmentalists, and even Nazis."

Sarah really hoped he wouldn't go off on the Nazi track with the general. Though Hank's concerns might be based on facts, his conspiracy theories sounded preposterous. "We don't know who's responsible," she said.

"If I've brought this danger into your home, I'm

sorry." He took her hand in both of his and gave a gentle squeeze. "We should have had the wedding at our place."

Rebecca gave him a fond, indulgent smile. "Apparently, the Nazis don't have our address."

"Senator, I have a way you can be helpful," Blake said. "Have you ever run a snowblower?"

Hank brightened. "I'm good with machinery."

"Get your jacket, and we'll get started."

"This is the kind of Western experience I wanted," Hank said, "being outdoors and battling the elements."

"Don't be late for dinner," Rebecca said. She handed the maid of honor dress to Sarah. "You should try this on tonight."

Before Blake left the room with the senator, he gave her a grin. "I can't wait to see you in the gown, princess."

All she needed was a tiara...and glass slippers.

Chapter Fourteen

At ten o'clock, Sarah stood in front of the mirror on her bathroom door admiring the liquid flow of emerald satin when she whirled to the right and looked over her shoulder. The gown didn't show a lot of skin, and the long sleeves were fitted all the way to the wrist with a series of tiny, pearl buttons that had been really hard to fasten. Another set of buttons went up the fitted bodice over her breasts. The satin draped from a high waist. An Empire waist? Her cousin Gabriella could have told her. Sarah whirled again. By definition, the maid of honor dress shouldn't outshine the bride, but this floor-length gown was spectacular.

She'd brushed her hair to a high sheen and swept it up into a loose ponytail that she'd fastened with an antique silver clip. After trying several necklaces and earrings, she'd decided that none of her clunky turquoise-and-silver jewelry looked right. This gown begged for something as sparkling and precious as the crown jewels.

Throughout the evening and dinner, Blake had been dropping princess references every time he got her alone. In the pantry when he was helping her carry the pies for dessert, he'd said, "I want to see you in that dress."

"You'll have to wait until the ceremony."

"There's no rule against seeing the maid of honor before the wedding."

"I guess not."

"Tonight," he said, "around ten."

She hoped she hadn't misinterpreted his cues about getting all dressed up. If she opened the door to her bedroom and found him standing there in sweatpants, it was going to be a major disappointment.

She watched as the numbers on the digital bedside clock flashed on ten. What if he didn't come at all? It wouldn't be the first time her fantasies had outpaced reality. When it came to love and relationships, she was better at imagining what could have been. Only once had she lived with a guy. That romance ended when her semester at college was over and she came back home for the summer. She'd never had a serious relationship while she was running the B and B, probably because she was too busy and too bossy.

One of her greatest fears was that she'd never leave Bentley's, that she'd grow old here—old, withered and alone. It had been different with her mom because she married young and always had her husband to stand beside her. Dad had been smart enough to work outside the B and B as an English teacher at the high school. Before they left, he'd worried that they were giving Sarah too much responsibility too soon. He'd like to see her settled down with a couple of kids of her own.

The numbers on the clock showed 10:10 p.m. She paced to the window, where the snow seemed to have abated, then crossed the room without looking in the mirror.

When she heard a rap on the door, she gasped. Practical pessimism told her not to expect too much. But she wanted to believe this would be a magical night, wanted so badly to believe.

Her hand rested on the doorknob. Her fingers were trembling. She yanked it open.

Blake stood there in a black suit with a white shirt and a striped silk necktie. In one hand, he held a bottle of Burgundy wine and two glasses with stems. In the other, he held a vibrant red rose. He clicked his heels and bowed.

"May I come in, Sarah?"

Speechless, she took a couple of steps backward. Unaccustomed to high heels, her feet were clumsy. Nonetheless, she bobbed a curtsy. "Welcome."

Her bedroom was the largest in the house, decorated in shades of slate-blue and cream. Like every room, it had hardwood floors and area rugs and was spotlessly clean. A beaded little chandelier over the bed added a sense of feminine whimsy. Her queen-size bed frame was dark wood, carved with antique-looking curlicues, and there was a cozy reading chair in one corner. Beside the window that looked out toward the front entrance, there was a small round table where she sometimes sat and had her morning coffee. He placed the wine and glasses on the table.

She didn't recognize the label on the bottle. It wasn't from her stock. "Where did you get that?"

"From a family vineyard in France," he said. "I was going to take it to the bachelor party, but I think beer goes better with strippers. And I wanted something special for you."

He placed the red rose beside the wine and turned to her. He took each of her hands and held them wide as his gaze swept from her head to her toes. "You're beautiful."

Happiness bubbled up inside her. She could feel a warm flush spreading from her throat to her cheeks. She felt beautiful. "Thank you."

"And the dress isn't half-bad."

"I thought you might be wearing your uniform," she said.

"Didn't bring it. Jeremy and I decided we'd go with regular suits." He hesitated. "I'm glad you caught my hint about the gown. I must have stood on the other side of your bedroom door for five minutes before I got up the courage to knock."

"Why would you be nervous?"

Still holding both her hands, he moved her around the room. "I've been in the army for a long time, much of it deployed. I haven't had much experience with proper relationships."

"Only the improper ones? A different woman in every port?"

"That's a myth."

"Really?"

"Mostly a myth," he said. "Now that I'm close to being retired, I see things differently. I want tonight to be something to remember."

He settled her in the padded chair beside the table, and she carefully smoothed the satin across her lap. "Well, here we are. All dressed up with nowhere to go."

"Where would you like to be?" he asked.

"Someplace far away and exotic."

He produced a Swiss Army knife with a corkscrew attachment and went to work on the bottle. "It's a great idea for you to travel. You could write it off as promotional expense."

"And who would run this place while I was gone?"

"You could find somebody to take over for a couple of weeks."

It was true. She could work something out. Her

exile at Bentley's B and B was mostly self-imposed. "Where's the best hotel you've ever stayed?"

He opened the wine and poured. "The most opulent was in Morocco, with soaring ceilings, high arches and mosaics in exotic colors. The food was rich, fresh and beautifully prepared."

"Just like my blueberry muffins."

He lifted his glass in a toast. "Here's to being exactly where I want to be right now."

"With exactly the right clothes," she added.

"And the perfect company."

He sat in the chair opposite her, and they talked while they sipped the rich red wine. Blake had traveled all over the world and had a great eye for details. He said he'd given up taking photos because he wanted to experience the sounds and smells and tastes.

When she looked down and saw the pearl wrist buttons of her emerald gown, she was struck by how strange it was that they were having this civilized conversation. They'd been in danger together. He'd seen her wearing a bra on her head. She'd honked his nose. But their conversation felt like opening the pages of a book, getting to know each other beyond the first impressions. She heard the warmth in his voice when he talked about his family and the sorrow when he spoke of fallen comrades.

And she told him all about her strange family

history, starting in the mid-1800s with the bigamous Frenchman. Some of her projects with her nonprofit organization to preserve the forest seemed dull until he pointed out that learning new conservation tactics gave her another reason to travel.

"To the next destination." She raised her wineglass in another toast. "You've probably had your fill of travel."

"Just because I'm retiring doesn't mean I plan to spend the rest of my life sitting in a rocking chair on the porch. I'm only thirty-five. I need a second career."

"What do you have in mind?"

"The stuff that's happened around here over the past few days has given me some ideas."

"Law enforcement," she guessed. "You'd be a good deputy or a detective. What did you hear from Kovak?"

"Franks is still unconscious, but the detectives in Denver have some background. He's divorced, lives alone and he owns a couple of businesses, including a shooting range and gun shop."

She shuddered. "Do you think he's a gun nut going after the senator?"

"We won't know until he wakes up and starts talking. And there's one more thing. Ten days ago, he had a twenty-five-thousand-dollar deposit from a bank in the Caymans."

"Someone hired him to do the kidnapping."

"Franks said he was scared of the person who hired him. That doesn't mean much. He's a cowardly little weasel."

"An offshore bank account sounds like big-time." She was imagining crime bosses and international thugs.

"But they didn't pay top dollar. And Franks isn't the best hit man money can buy."

Sipping her wine, she listened as he drifted from one thought to another in a sort of free association. His deep voice was soothing and exciting at the same time. She asked, "Your conclusion?"

"This isn't an organized threat. We're dealing with someone who used Franks to reach out and take a slap."

"Why would anyone do this?" When he reached out with the wine bottle, she waved him off. She'd had just enough to feel pleasantly intoxicated. "What did they hope to accomplish with a bomb?"

"Pain," he said as he finished off his wine. "Bombs are meant to cause damage and inflict pain."

He stood and stretched. His long arms reached the ceiling. While they had been talking, he'd loosened his necktie. He reached out toward her. "If there was music, I'd ask you to dance."

"I can take care of that."

Using a remote control, she turned on her private sound system that was set to play the classical music she used to fall asleep. The volume was set to low and she turned it up a bit. She wasn't worried about disturbing the other guests. The only other people staying in this wing were Emily and Jeremy, and they were so wrapped up in being together that Sarah could have set off fireworks and they wouldn't notice.

Blake took her in his arms as the lilting cadence of a waltz filled the bedroom. Her head tilted back and she gazed into his deep blue eyes. Even in her high heels, she was considerably shorter than he was. He twirled her in the limited space and lowered her into a dip. His face was only inches from hers. Leaning down, he lightly kissed her lips.

When he pulled her upright, she rested her cheek against his shoulder and closed her eyelids. Her imagination spun a fantasy of a ballroom filled with mirrors and every surface reflected her emerald gown. Tonight was magical, and she had a feeling that it was about to get better.

He lifted her off her feet for a twirl, and then placed her on the edge of her bed. Kneeling before her, he took off her right shoe and glided his hand up her ankle and down to her arch. He did the same with the other foot. She was Cinderella in reverse.

She patted the bed beside her. "Join me."

Before she knew what was happening, they were

stretched out on her quilt, side by side. “Be careful of the dress,” she said. “I don’t want to wreck it before the ceremony.”

“You’re right. We should probably take it off.” The fairy tale was about to turn real. Though she hadn’t planned it this way, she was ready to make love. Lying on her back, she held up her wrists as though she was wearing manacles. “Undo these buttons first. They’re complicated.”

“Not yet.”

He leaned over her. Without touching the dress, he kissed her. His lips slid across hers, and he tasted sweet like the Burgundy wine. She arched toward him, yearning to feel his body against hers but not wanting to wrinkle the gown. With her tongue, she traced the line of his full lower lip.

The strains of classical violins urged her toward more contact, but he held her down as he straddled her body, again being careful not to wrinkle the dress. He lifted her wrist and unfastened the tiny pearl buttons. Holding her gaze, he did the other sleeve. Then he pinned both arms above her head and thoroughly kissed her again.

Excitement raced through her blood. *Forget about the dress.* She wanted him, needed to feel the weight of his big, masculine body pressed against hers. She struggled to free her arms.

“Not so fast,” he said. “I want to savor the moment. I’ve wanted this for a long time.”

What was he talking about? "It's only been a few days, a few hours."

"All my life," he whispered in her ear. "I've been waiting for you all my life."

She wasn't sure what that meant, but she liked the way it sounded. She tried to sit up and show him how much she liked it, but he held her in place. He'd been a perfect gentleman while they were talking. Now he was taking her to a different place, and he was clearly in control. "What do you want from me, Blake?"

"Lie still."

Though every atom, every muscle in her body craved his touch, she forced herself to lie quietly while he unfastened the tiny buttons on her bodice. Under his touch, the dress loosened and opened, revealing her black lace bra.

With seemingly little effort, he lifted her from the bed and settled her feet on the floor beside the bed.

Her knees were shaky as she stood before him. Carefully, he pulled her arms from the sleeves and lifted the garment over her head. He tossed the emerald satin over the back of a chair and focused entirely on her.

"This isn't fair." Her voice was breathless. "You're still dressed."

"And you're still beautiful." He held her hands wide, the same way he'd done when she was wearing her gown. His blue eyes admired her in her black bra and matching panties. When he pulled her closer, her heart leaped inside her rib cage. She was breathing harder than if she'd run a mile.

With an incredibly skillful touch, he caressed her shoulders and her waist. His hands rose to cup her breasts and flick at the taut nipples. Shivers of pure delight chased across her skin.

Her arms clung to him. Her mouth pressed against his, demanding more kisses. Never in her life had she wanted a man so much. She ached with her need for him.

Again, he took control, placing her on the bed. He loomed over her as he tore off his jacket, then his tie and his white shirt. His chest was broad and muscular with a mat of hair that begged to be touched. She noticed a long, jagged scar on his left shoulder. Gasping, she asked, "The scar. What happened?"

"Battle."

Reaching down, he removed the holster clipped to his belt. A simple gesture but a reminder of the dangerous life he'd led. He was always prepared for armed conflict, even while they were going to bed. The man was a warrior. Not the type she'd ever expected to wind up with.

His trousers fell from his hips, followed by his boxers. Magnificently naked, he joined her on the bed. Their bodies molded together. All restraint was gone.

He threw one leg over her, and she bucked against him in passionate struggle. Her touch was greedy, kneading at his muscles and sliding down his torso until she grasped his sex. He reacted with a growl.

He tore open her front-fastened bra and nuzzled at her breasts. His hand creased her belly and dipped lower, finding the edge of her panties. He reached inside. She was moist and ready for him.

Desperate need pounded through her, consuming her practical logic and her fantasies, as well. She wanted him inside her, wanted him to be a part of her. Though she wasn't thinking of condoms, she was glad when he slipped one on.

Poised above her, he gazed into her eyes, making contact and sending a message. "Sarah," he whispered. "All my life, I've been looking for you."

"I can't wait anymore," she cried. "Take me."

"You're mine."

With his knees, he nudged her legs apart and entered her. He paused halfway, and she writhed beneath him, wanting all of him. Inch by inch, he penetrated her fully.

Her body wrapped around him, demanding and savoring every hard thrust. Fireworks were already exploding in her peripheral vision, but she didn't stop. Nor did he. Arching over her, he pushed her to the peak of sensation. She poised at the verge. And then came the release.

Shuddering from head to toe, she collapsed on the bed. His words echoed in her ears. He had been waiting for her all his life. And she was glad he'd found her.

Chapter Fifteen

The next morning, Blake carried an armload of wood from the mudroom to the wood bin by the fireplace, mindfully handling the responsibility Sarah had given him. After last night, he wanted to do everything for her, from brushing her hair to washing the dishes. They'd made love three times, each better than the time before, and he couldn't think of anything but her. How the hell was he going to leave her on Sunday? The simple answer: he wasn't.

There was another week before his next assignment and no reason why he couldn't spend it with her. If he called in some favors, he could wrangle another few days on top of that. Even better than staying here would be if he could convince Sarah to come away with him, to take one of the vacations she'd dreamed about. He was ready to ask if he ever got a chance to talk to her alone. When he woke this morning, she was already out of the bed, and she hadn't stopped running since then.

Every time he got close, they were interrupted. It was almost as though she was avoiding him.

Squatting at the fireplace, he fed another log into the blaze. Outside near the front porch, the senator and Skip were taking turns with the snowblower, clearing the entrance and parking lot. Last night, another four or five inches had accumulated.

Alvardo and Maddox stood at the front window, looking out. Maddox had taken charge of the camera feeds and the screen was never far from his grasp. The Reuben twins patrolled the area, reporting to Maddox on walkie-talkies.

Alvardo said, "The forecast is calling for ten to twelve more inches. Do you think we'll be snowed in?"

"Sarah has a contract with a local guy who has a snowplow on his truck," Blake said. "He'll try to keep the roads clear, but if the snow starts coming down heavy, we'll be stuck. Is that a problem?"

"Not as long as we can make our flight on Sunday morning. I can still use the computer with the landline modem, and I've vetted everybody who's coming to the house today. That includes the cake baker, the caterer and his two helpers and, of course, the stripper."

"What's her name again?" Maddox asked. His goofy grin made him look as eager as a teenager.

"Honey Buxom," Alvardo said. "A blonde belly dancer."

"I'm glad that's taken care of," Blake said without much enthusiasm. He wasn't a huge fan of bachelor parties, especially not with the diverse group of people staying here.

Alvardo leered. "If she's anywhere as sexy in person as she sounded on the phone, we're in for a treat."

"Did you go out for your run this morning?"

He nodded. "Just a quick run. I'm on my way to the treadmill in the game room to get in the rest of my exercise."

The general descended the staircase and nodded to him. "Blake, come with me."

Together, they went down the hallway to Sarah's office, where the general took the position of authority behind the desk. He didn't waste words. "I want more information on Norman Franks, specifically on his gun shop."

"I spoke to Kovak this morning." It irked Blake that his best telephone connection with the deputy had been through Sarah's landline. His satellite phones utilized space-age technology, but the thick cloud cover and the snow made the old-fashioned system the most effective. "The firing range and gun shop—Frank's Firearms—are a relatively small part of his business. Mostly, he's a landlord who owns several low-rent buildings in east Denver."

"What about restaurants?" The general leaned back in the swivel desk chair. "Or import-export concerns?"

"Kovak didn't mention anything like that. The Denver detective called him an opportunist—a guy who finances other people and walks away with a chunk of the profit."

"That's the sort of investigating I need—a local cop, boots on the ground, poking around and asking questions about associates. We've already got the computer data. Alvardo did a detailed background search using classified information."

The general's resources went far and deep. A classified source might mean Homeland Security or CIA. "And?"

"Franks has a tie to the illegal gun trade in the Middle East. He's not one of the bosses, not a kingpin."

"I didn't have that impression of him," Blake said. Cowardly weasel was a description that suited Franks just fine. "He was quick to back down when we took his hired thugs into custody. And he surrendered as soon as Jeremy and I had him surrounded."

"I don't want to make too much of this." The

general stood. "I'm not like that hothead, Hank Layton, seeing conspiracy theories behind every shrub."

The two men had been doing a semi-believable job of getting along, even if it was only a show for Emily and her mother. "What are you saying, General?"

"Franks isn't our problem, but his bosses might be. He could be working for some high-powered gunrunners."

"Terrorists?" Blake hated the word and all it implied. In spite of the initial gunplay and the explosive device in the backpack, he'd been treating Franks as a fairly low-level threat. "If we're dealing with international gunrunners, we should get the hell out of here before we get snowed in."

"Don't get your panties in a bunch," the general growled. "Alvardo did the research and he's good at his job. The connection to Franks is tenuous at best."

"What's the worst-case scenario?" Blake asked.

"I believe Franks has already fulfilled his purpose. He was sent to deliver a message."

"Which is?"

"I'm not safe. My family isn't safe."

Blake's thoughts went immediately to Sarah. If anything happened to her or to the B and B, he'd never forgive himself. "Have you received other such messages?"

"All the time." His voice was weary. "Ninety percent are all talk and no action."

That left a worrisome 10 percent.

The general massaged the heavy creases on his forehead. "I trust Alvardo's sources. He says we're okay."

Blake didn't feel comfortable about putting their safety in the hands of Alvardo—an obsessive, ambitious Pentagon officer working his way up the ladder. "The next time Kovak calls, I'll ask about possible Middle East connections."

"You do that." He swiveled around to face the desktop and turned on the computer. "I'll see what I can find from this end. And if Senator Hank starts babbling about a pro-gun lobby tracking him down, just mention Area 51. That'll distract him. Alien invasion trumps survivalists."

Maddox poked his head into the room. "Sir, there's a vehicle approaching on the road. A white van."

"What else can you tell me?" Blake asked.

"The sign on the side says Belle's Bakery."

In the kitchen, Blake tracked down Sarah. She was working with two other women on a fried chicken lunch. When she saw him, her dark eyes glistened. It seemed to him that she was glowing, but she didn't draw him aside into that handy little alcove beside the pantry for a quick kiss. Had he done something last night to tick her off?

"This is the last meal I have to worry about," she announced. "After lunch, these wonderful ladies are going home, and the caterers are responsible for feeding everybody."

"Great." He reached toward her, but she moved away. "There's a van coming up the—"

"Wish I could stay for that catered dinner," one of the ladies said. Her name, he remembered, was Carrie. "Crab cakes and that beef dish with mushrooms. Yum."

"The general picked the menu," Sarah said.

The other woman—a tiny creature with frizzy gray hair—fussed at the sink. "I need to get home and batten down the hatches. We're in for a blizzard."

"They say it's going to be worse than the blizzard in '04. I couldn't get out of my house for three days."

"At least the ski areas are happy."

Their chatter created a shield around Sarah, making it difficult for him to get closer until her handmaidens moved away. Was she trying to be hard to get? That wasn't like her. She wasn't someone who played games.

A commotion at the back door drew her attention, and she flew to unlock the door.

A bulky woman who must have been Belle the baker, because that was what it said on the back of her hot-pink parka, tromped in from the snow.

Her van was parked as close to the door as possible. Though he offered to help, she and her helper did the unloading. They carried a flat board with a two-foot-high box centered on it. When they had it placed on a rear counter, Belle carefully lifted the cardboard to reveal a three-tier cake with red rose and lily decorations.

While Sarah and the other two ladies made appropriate oohs and ahhs, Belle dug into the pocket of her parka and took out tiny figures of the bride and groom, which she placed on the top tier.

"Wait until you taste," Belle said. "It's red velvet with cream custard filling, dark chocolate with peanut butter mousse and French vanilla with mint mocha."

"You've outdone yourself." Sara turned to Blake and continued, "Belle is famous for the fancy cakes she makes for the celebs in Aspen."

"But I always save the best for the locals." Instead of turning around and heading back to her truck, Belle unzipped her parka, strode up to him and gave him a long, hard look. "Are you the handsome groom I've heard so much about?"

"Only the best man," Blake said.

"Ah, yes. Dolly at the Laughing Dog told me all about you. A great big army ranger, she said. Pretty blue eyes, she said. You and our Sarah are an item."

Blake didn't have pretty blue eyes in the back of

his head, but he could feel the other two women gesturing behind his back for Belle to keep quiet. Everybody in a small town knew everybody else's business, and Sarah was a native daughter. They were all concerned about her, protecting her. From him?

He'd had enough. If Sarah wanted to play games, he'd show her how it was done. He confronted Belle. "I guess you could say we're an item."

Three smiles encouraged him. Carrie the cook said, "You look real cute together."

He focused directly on her. "I was thinking of inviting Sarah on a vacation, a trip to Puerto Vallarta."

"In Mexico?" Carrie clapped her hands together. "I love it. I'll take care of the B and B."

"Hold on," Sarah said. "There's no need to make plans."

"You'd better take that offer." Belle clapped Blake on the back. "Or I will."

"Can't go to Mexico," Sarah said. "Don't have a passport."

He enjoyed watching her squirm. "If not Mexico, how about New Orleans?"

"For Mardi Gras," Carrie said. "Sarah, you have to go."

Through tight lips, she said, "Will you ladies excuse us?"

She hooked her arm through his and dragged

him into the mudroom. Here, away from the stove, it was colder. Through the windows, he saw the snow coming down more heavily. In spite of the senator's efforts with the snowblower, the area between the garage and the house was piling up with fresh snowfall.

Sarah closed the door to the kitchen. Through the glass window in the door, she could still see her friends watching with well-meaning interest.

"We need more privacy." She shoved open a painted door that opened onto a staircase going down. "This way."

With all his exploring and checking security, he'd been in the basement only twice, never through this access staircase. Plain concrete stretched from one end of the house to the other in the rough, unfinished basement. Directly in front of them was a laundry, equipped with extra-large machines, tables for folding and bins for storing the sheets and towels. Other shelves held what looked like camping gear. There was a furnace, wires, pipes, two water heaters and a generator.

He asked, "Do you always leave this door unlocked?"

"Does it matter if the outside door is locked?"

His conversation with the general about terrorists had heightened his awareness of the threat. "It might."

She braced her fists on her hips and looked up

at him. "You can't just spring a trip to Mexico on me."

"Come to think of it, I like the idea of New Orleans better. It's going to be tough to get reservations for Mardi Gras, but I know a guy."

"Stop it," she snapped. "I don't want to go to New Orleans, either."

"I would have asked for your dream destination this morning, but you were already out of bed when I woke up."

"Is that what this is about? You're mad because I got up early to make muffins."

"I wasn't angry before, but I'm getting there." He squared off to confront her. "Here's the deal, princess. I don't like playing games."

"Neither do I," she said.

"Why are you avoiding me?"

"I'm not."

But she was, and she knew it. If he walked into a room, she went out the other side. She kept other people standing between them like sentries. "Tell me the truth."

Her dark eyes blazed. "The first person I saw this morning was Emily, who wanted details, details, details. You know what? I didn't feel like sharing. Last night belongs to me and to you. Nobody else needs to know what happened. Everybody gets in my face about dating and getting married and it's my business. My private business."

"And mine."

"And you're right. I have been avoiding you, running away and hiding and putting off this moment." Her fingers laced together in a knot. "I might pretend to be a princess, but that's not me. I'm realistic. Last night was magic. But it wasn't a promise or an obligation. It's over. You'll go your way, and I'll stay right here."

"What if I don't want to leave?"

"Don't tease me, Blake. It's not funny."

"I'm not laughing." He saw a shimmer in her eyes. Tears? "Don't cry, princess. I like you."

She held his face in her hands and kissed him with a raw, passionate desire. Her tongue penetrated his mouth and tangled with his. When she pulled away, she caught his lower lip between her teeth and gave a tug.

"That's how I feel about you," she whispered. "I can't put it in words. I don't know what to say. Everything has happened so fast, and I'm scared."

Her vulnerability touched him. It had taken a lot for her to admit her fear. "There's nothing to be afraid of."

"But you're leaving on Sunday."

"I can adjust my schedule," he said. "I want to stay with you, at least for a couple of weeks."

With a sigh, she melted into his arms. Her soft curves fit so perfectly against him that she could have been created only for him. He had a strong feeling that two more weeks with her wasn't going to be enough.

The door from the upstairs opened. Alvardo called down, "Is Sarah down there?"

"I'm here," she answered without moving away from Blake.

"We have a problem," Alvardo said. "The computer modem doesn't work. Your landline phones are dead."

"It happens," she said. "The snow weighs down the lines and they break."

"What am I supposed to do?"

"Wait it out." She tilted her head back and looked up at Blake. "I guess that makes it official. We're snowed in."

Chapter Sixteen

As far as Sarah was concerned, having the phone lines go down was an inconvenience they could live with for a few days. But a couple of her guests—Alvardo and Skip—had worked themselves into a near panic and insisted on an emergency meeting before lunch. Everyone, including Ollie and the Dewdrops, gathered around the dining room table.

"No computer, no Wi-Fi, no phone line," Skip said. You would have thought his lifelines had been cut and he'd been cast adrift. "How are we supposed to do business?"

"You're not," Blake said. "It's noon on Friday, and you're leaving on Sunday. Business will have to wait until then."

"It's like the good old days," Hank said as he leaned back in his chair and took his wife's hand. "Most of our conversations were face-to-face. You didn't have to limit your word count. And you could see how someone reacted."

"The old ways were better," the general said. "I don't mind living without computers at all."

"Finally," Rebecca said, "there's something we can agree on."

Alvardo cast a dark look toward Sarah. "Is there any way to repair the landline?"

"Sorry," she said. "If the line is down, the phone company will have to come out to repair it. That won't be happening with the blizzard."

Outside, the snow was accumulating inch by inch. She was worried that the caterer wouldn't be able to get through, and she'd have to figure out how to feed everybody from her stores in the pantry. At least they had the cake and the flowers.

Alvardo wasn't about to give up. "What about the satellite phone?"

Blake held up his phone for illustration. "Reception has been spotty all day. Right now, I've got no signal at all."

"How can that be?" Skip rose from the table and waved his hands. "Aren't those things supposed to work in the Arctic? Aren't they infallible?"

"They're pretty damn good," Blake said. "There might be a problem with the terminal I placed outside. I suppose I could take a hike and check it out."

"I'll come with you," Skip said.

"I'd rather you keep working with the snowblower," Sarah said. "You and Hank are doing a great job, and I really need to keep the area around the kitchen cleared for the caterer."

Rebecca spoke for her husband. "Sorry, Sarah, Hank has made his last pass with the snowblower. He's been having fun with it, but he's pooped. We're California people."

"Nonsense," he said. "I'm not tired."

"Sweetheart, it makes me exhausted just to look at you. Sarah, is there anything else we can do to be helpful?"

Her greatest concern was the power lines. If they lost electricity, it was going to be seriously inconvenient. She had an emergency generator, but it hadn't been used in years. Depending on the generator meant they'd have to cut down on electricity use—limiting hot water for showers and closing off some of the rooms. Later this afternoon, she'd make sure there were working flashlights in all the bedrooms.

She studied the array of worried faces around the dining room table. There was no point in bringing up a problem that might never happen. "Everything is going to be fine."

One of Ollie's Dewdrops made a suggestion. "We could bring our instruments down here and have a mini-concert."

"That would be lovely," Emily said as she rose to her feet. "After lunch we could play board games."

When Rebecca looked up at her daughter and

grinned, the family resemblance was evident. Not so much in the physical sense, but Sarah could see where Emily got her boundless optimism.

"I like a good board game," the general said, "especially that one where you take over the world."

"How about a game of chess?" Hank asked.

"You're on, Senator."

"I should warn you," Hank said. "I was on the chess team at Stanford."

"I beat the secretary of the navy. Strategy is my game."

"We'll see."

Sarah pushed away from the table. "Lunch will be in half an hour."

In the kitchen, she saw Carrie unlocking the door for Slim Martinez, the caterer. Unlike his name, Slim was a big man in every sense of the word. His voice boomed, "The roads, *Dios mio,* the roads are hell. We almost crashed."

"It's true," said his assistant who was also his son, Ramon. "It's ice under the snow."

"Should have let me drive," said the second assistant, Slim's daughter, Marisol.

"I'm so glad you're here." Sarah clasped Marisol's hands. She and her brother were well-trained in the kitchen and incredibly good-looking. Both had long, shining black hair pulled back in a ponytail at the nape. Both were slender and graceful, which was only one of the reasons why Slim Martinez Catering was in high demand. His food was to die for.

"The roads," Slim wailed again. He burst forth with a rapid-fire stream of Spanish. Sarah could pick out only every third word, but Blake was able to answer Slim and ask questions.

"Papa," Marisol chided. "In English."

"Muy malo," Slim said. "It's snowing like hell."

Sarah had suspected as much. Not only was the snow coming faster but the winds had picked up. The local guy who did the snow plowing had made his last run about an hour ago, and his work was almost erased. No matter what happened, loading her guests into trucks and vans and attempting the drive to a hotel in Aspen was out of the question. They were stuck here for the duration of the blizzard.

GROWING UP IN WISCONSIN, Blake was accustomed to cold and snow. He'd skied, he'd snowboarded and he'd tasted his first beer on a daylong ice fishing expedition with his dad. When he left the B and B with Sarah after lunch to check the spot where he'd placed the terminal for the satellite phone, he was dressed for subzero temperatures. And he was armed.

His handgun was inside his parka, and he had a rifle attached with a sling across his chest. Through snow goggles, he scanned the forest surrounding the B and B. His camera surveillance was pretty much worthless in the storm, but he doubted anyone would attack during the blizzard. Just in case, he'd stationed the twins and Maddox—who was turning out to be a much more useful soldier than Alvardo—in vantage points to keep watch. And they had plenty of other people who could take up arms.

Under the eaves at the south end of the B and B, Sarah stood beside him. Though the wind was blowing from the north, the snow had drifted halfway up to the window ledges. In her parka with the hood pulled up and snow goggles in place, she was so covered up that only a glimpse of her face was visible.

"I'm glad Carrie and her friend left," she said. "Within the hour, the road coming down to the B and B is going to be impassable."

"We've got everybody here who needs to be here."

"Not quite," she said. "We're missing the justice of the peace."

"I can do the ceremony," he said.

"You?"

"I got one of those online certifications when I was in Afghanistan. One of the guys in my squad wanted to get married, and I did the ceremony on Skype. Apart from the kissing the bride part, it was kind of romantic."

"You're kind of romantic," she said.

Being sentimental didn't fit with his image as a ranger, but he knew it was true. Not that he cried at chick flicks or got all goopy about birthdays and such. But he loved a happy ending. After one particularly bloody debriefing, the army shrink told him that he'd seen too much sorrow, pain and tragedy. Blake needed to believe that things would turn out all right in the end.

Like with Sarah.

He was glad that she'd volunteered to come with him. She was the obvious choice since she knew her way around these hills better than anyone else, but she could have refused. Last night, she'd been the beautiful, pampered princess. Today, she was practical Sarah slogging through the blizzard.

"Which way do we go?" she asked.

"I wanted to set the terminal as high as possible." He pointed. "Up that slope and into the trees."

"Couldn't you just put it on the roof?"

"The B and B is tucked away in the trees. I wanted a clear view."

He led the way, crossing an open area through snow that was nearly up to his knees while she walked in his tracks. The wind from the north drove the snow nearly horizontal, straight into his face. The parka, gloves and cap kept him warm enough, but he could feel moisture seeping into his jeans and his boots. His feet were going to be ice cubes by the time they got back to the B and B.

When they entered the forest, the force of the storm was buffered by the trees. He looked up. Visibility was a problem, even with his snow goggles. "I wedged the terminal in the branches of a pine tree, a little higher than eye level."

"Plenty of trees," she said. "Any idea which one?"

"Up higher." He felt her tug at his arm, and he turned toward her. "What is it?"

"I heard something. A whining noise."

He listened for a moment. He heard the wind and nothing more. "Do you still hear it?"

"I guess not." She shook her head. "Did Kovak ever find the snowmobile that Franks used?"

"Yeah, he did. It was a rental." Blake clapped his hands together to get his circulation going. "It'd be handy to have a snowmobile right now."

"I was just thinking that we should have worn snowshoes." She pointed to her lower legs. "Even with you going first, my snow pants are wet up to the knees."

"Waterproof snow pants," he scoffed. "I'm wearing jeans."

She grinned. "You can handle it. You're a big, tough ranger."

"No sympathy from you?"

"Not a smidge." She turned him around and

gave his backside a shove. "Let's hurry up and find your terminal tree. I want to get back to the house and sit by the fireplace."

"When we get back, I've got a better way to keep you warm."

"You wish," she teased.

He hiked a few paces higher on a steep hill, slipping on the icy rocks hidden beneath the snow. If he could have seen the landmark shapes of rocks and trees, he would have known where he was going. Instead, he relied on a natural sense of direction that he'd had since childhood.

A long time ago, he'd learned that if he trusted his instincts he'd always be able to find his way. Before he left for his first deployment in the Middle East, his mom had reminded him to believe in himself and find his way home.

He'd thought of those words many times. He'd lived by them.

Turning to his right, he dug in the toe of his boot to go uphill. "It's over here."

At the top of a ridge, the trees thinned and the wind picked up. He saw the pine tree with an outstretched branch like an arm that should have been cradling the terminal for his satellite phones. "It's gone."

She stopped beside him. "Are you sure this is the right tree?"

Reaching up, he brushed the snow off the

branch. The outer bark had been broken when he wedged the terminal box into place. On the ground, he found one of the bungee cords he'd used to fasten the terminal to the tree. "It was here."

She looked over her shoulder. "The wind is pretty fierce up here. It might have knocked the terminal out of the tree."

"A nine-pound box didn't walk away by itself."

His satellite phone had been sabotaged. And it wasn't Franks who did it because Blake had used the phone this morning. Someone had gone to a hell of a lot of trouble to cut off his communications.

That someone could be nearby, watching them through the infrared sight of a rifle. Peering through his goggles, he scanned the surrounding landscape. If there had been a sniper, he would have already taken his shot. Or would he?

Blake bent from the waist, brushing the snow from his parka, and studied the ground for footprints or tracks. Sarah did the same. Though the wind and snow had likely erased any sign of what had happened, he kept looking.

She walked downhill, studying the ground. "Over here, it looks like something flat was pushed through the snow."

"Like the terminal," he said.

Stepping onto a jutting rock, she peered over the edge. "Found it."

On the rocks below them, rapidly being covered by the drifting snow, was the satellite phone terminal box. From what he could see, the box appeared to be pretty much intact. He lowered himself down the rocks so he could pick it up.

"What do you think happened?" she asked.

"I'd like to think that a bear knocked the terminal out of the tree and played with it until it fell off the cliff."

"I'd like that, too."

But that wasn't what had happened. "I'd have to say that the terminal was sabotaged."

"Who would have known it was here?"

That was the difficult part of the question. He was certain that he hadn't been observed when he first rigged the terminal in the tree. The next day, when blowing snow hadn't been a factor, someone must have gone on a search. Finding the terminal wouldn't have been too difficult. Anyone who knew about satellite phones would know it needed to be at a high point.

He reached down for the box and picked it up. There was a bullet hole in the dead center.

He called back up to her, "It wasn't a bear."

Chapter Seventeen

As Sarah followed Blake into the sheltering trees near the B and B, she noticed that he'd taken off his heavy gloves and was only wearing the liners. His right hand cradled the Glock he'd been carrying in his holster. They were in danger. She couldn't deny it. The shiver that went down her spine wasn't entirely due to the frigid temperature. She felt as if they were caught in a trap and the escape routes were being cut off one by one.

They'd left the damaged box where it was. Looking up at him, she asked, "What do we tell people about the terminal?"

"We're going to have to say that we looked but couldn't find it. Don't talk about this with anyone—not even Emily."

"Why?"

"The box was sabotaged. I've been asking myself who did it, and I can only see two possibilities—someone working with Franks from the outside, or someone on the inside."

A traitor among them. She couldn't believe it. "But Alvardo checked all their records."

"Think about it," he said. "Someone in the house could monitor all our activities. Before the snow hit, they had plenty of time to locate the terminal, and they could have slipped out this morning to destroy it."

"The cameras would have shown them sneaking around."

"There's been plenty of time to study the camera feeds. They'd know how to avoid being caught in the picture."

The stark realization hit her. "They could be planning to hurt Emily or Jeremy. We have to get them out of here. I know the roads are bad, but it's safer for them to try an escape."

"If we do that, we're forcing his hand. He'll have to strike." Blake held her arm, anchoring her with his strength. "You need to stay calm, can't let him see that you're suspicious."

"I think I can do that." She was accustomed to handling a crisis without showing she was rattled, but this was different. This wasn't a case of noisy guest causing problems in the hallway late at night. Potentially, this was life and death.

"We need to identify our enemy," he said, "before we make our move. Right now, we have the advantage because he doesn't know we're looking for him."

Blake made the plan sound simple. To him, it was second nature to face enemies and assassins without blinking an eyelash. She wasn't anywhere near that cool. "Do you know anything more about this person? Is he an enemy of the general or the senator? Why is he doing this?"

"I don't have answers."

"What should I do?"

"Stay with Emily. Don't let her be alone. If he tries to grab her, you'll be in the way." He pulled her close for a quick hug. "I know you're scared. You'd be crazy not to worry. But you can't give in to it, okay? Stay calm. I'm going to make sure nothing bad happens. You have to trust me."

"I do."

Less than an hour ago, her greatest problem was figuring out their relationship. The threat to Emily and to everyone else was so much bigger.

She and Blake had barely gotten into the house and taken off their snow gear when the next crisis hit. She heard John Reuben call out, "Open the door. Get out there and help her."

Blake dashed through the kitchen to the front, and she followed. They saw both Reuben twins and Alvardo charging through the front door and onto the porch. When they stepped into the snow, it was up to their knees.

"What is it?" she asked Hank.

"A woman," he said. "She's trudging through

the snow. The poor thing looks like she's on her last legs."

John scooped the woman off her feet and carried her through the deep snow onto the porch and then into the house. She was wearing a bright yellow parka and a pink polka-dot backpack. When John placed her on the sofa, she leaned back and closed her eyes for a moment before she leaned forward. "I'm okay," she said. "Just a little cold."

Sarah naturally took over, sitting beside her and helping her take off her gloves and remove the backpack. "What are you doing out here?"

"I didn't think the snow was this bad. My little Subaru has four-wheel drive, and it's usually great. But I got stuck." Her lower lip trembled. "I think I'm blocking the road."

"Where did you leave your car?" Sarah asked.

"Not far from here. I skidded at the last turn leading in here."

Her abandoned Subaru wouldn't be a problem for anyone else on the road, but they couldn't get out without moving the vehicle. Their escape was cut off.

"I'm so sorry," the woman said. When she unzipped her parka and pushed back the hood, a cascade of platinum-blond curls fell nearly to her waist.

Sarah wanted to pull her hair and tell her that she was an idiot for driving in this weather, but

Alvardo was all over this lady. He sat beside her and took her hand. "It's all right."

"No," Sarah said angrily, "it's not all right. We need to move her car."

Ignoring Sarah, Alvardo continued to hold the woman's hand and speak gently. "I tried to reach you and tell you not to come, but all our phones were out."

"It's okay," she said with a whimper.

William Reuben handed her a bottled water. "Drink this."

"Thanks, sweetie." She gave them all a smile. "Pleased to meet you. I'm Honey Buxom."

Just what they needed.... A stripper.

AT SARAH'S INSISTENCE, the men went out to see if they could move Honey's vehicle. She noticed that when Blake organized their expedition, he chose Jeremy, of course. Then he took Maddox, Alvardo, Skip, Ramon Martinez and the three-man band. Were those men the most likely suspects? The choice of Ramon surprised her because he hadn't been at the B and B until a few hours ago, but she didn't question Blake's decision.

The group he left behind included the Reuben twins, the general, the senator and all the women. Rebecca had plans for them. "Ladies, come upstairs with me. We're going to have a spa day. Marisol, you're welcome to come along."

"Thank you, ma'am, but I'm sous chef for my papa. He'll never get the crab cakes right without me."

Rebecca smiled at the platinum-blonde stripper. "What about you? We're going to do mani-pedis, facials and hair treatments."

"Not the hair," Honey said. "I just got it done. But I could use a manicure."

Usually, Sarah didn't have the patience for beauty treatments. Facials made her itch. Manicures didn't last for more than a day. And she hated sitting still. But a spa day gave her a good reason to stay with Emily, and that was her goal. She meant to stick like superglue to her friend and make sure no one got close enough to threaten her.

Rebecca's wardrobe bedroom was directly across the hall from the last vacant room that Sarah had assigned to Honey and Marisol because she couldn't put the two women upstairs in the dormitory with the band and the other two caterers.

As soon as they were in the bedroom, the others stripped down to underwear and bathrobes. Sarah refused. "I need to be dressed in case there's some kind of emergency."

"You work so hard on this place," Rebecca said. "Don't forget to take time for yourself."

"From what I hear," Emily said, "she's taking the time…for a trip to New Orleans with Blake."

Gossip traveled at the speed of light. "Nothing has been decided," Sarah said.

"You'll go," Emily said. "Once Blake has his mind set, he doesn't give up. And he's set on you."

"You make it sound like I'm prey, and he's the hunter."

"In the game of love," Emily said with a boisterous grin.

Her level of cheerfulness was off the charts—a byproduct of spending time with Jeremy. And Emily's joy brightened everyone's mood. In spite of Sarah's fears, she found herself laughing with the other women as Rebecca mixed up a batch of green goop and started smearing it onto their faces.

Emily asked the stripper, "Are you new to the area?"

"I'm visiting friends," she said. "I might open a dance studio in Aspen."

"I'm sure you'd be successful," Rebecca said. "I have a friend who takes pole dancing classes. Not only does it keep her in shape, but her husband loves to watch her work out."

"Mom, please." Emily rolled her eyes. "I don't need to hear this from you."

"You might learn something. I'm a very sensual woman."

"I'm sure."

"Really," Rebecca said, "I've lived in San Francisco for twenty-five years, and I have a handsome husband in politics who never looks at another woman. So I must be doing something right."

"But Honey is the expert," Emily said. "How did you get into stripping?"

"Belly dancing," Honey corrected her. "My cousin taught me. She danced at many weddings and bachelor parties."

Though she looked like a cheap Kewpie doll and went by the name of Honey Buxom, the woman sounded a bit insulted by being called a stripper. She might have an interesting story. Up close without makeup, Honey looked like she was Sarah's age, in her thirties. "Have you been belly dancing for a long time?"

"Long enough," she said. "I've won many competitions. That was why Mr. Alvardo hired me. He looked me up on the internet."

I'll bet he did. "I wish we ladies had a chance to see you perform," Sarah said. "The bachelor party is all male."

"Show us some moves," Emily said.

"Very well."

Honey went into the bathroom and washed the goop from her face. When she emerged, she dropped one shoulder on her bathrobe, then the other. In her tan bra and panties, she appeared almost nude. Her state of undress didn't embarrass her in the least as she struck a dramatic pose with her weight on her left foot and her right toe pointed in front. Her arms arched gracefully over her head, and her head tilted back.

She had a terrific hourglass figure and a golden tan so perfect that it had to come from a salon. Her stomach was sucked in, and her rib cage stuck out.

"I move like this," she said as she thrust her pelvis to the right. She stepped forward. "Then like this." Another thrust.

In case they were getting the idea that belly dancing was easy, she went through a series of complex gyrations and belly rolls.

Sarah, Emily and Rebecca cheered. When Honey made a high-pitched trill, they all did the same. They circled her, clapping in time to her movements. The way she isolated muscle groups was astounding. While her hips were vibrating wildly, her upper body was completely still. Her big finish was to shudder all over and collapse to the floor with her long blond hair spread around her.

The other three women applauded.

"The men," Sarah said, "are never going to appreciate how much skill that takes. I can see why you won contests."

Her eyes, which were nearly as dark as Sarah's, glittered. "Thank you."

"If you get that dance studio set up, let me know. I'll be first in line to sign up for lessons."

Sarah wished they had access to the internet. She would have liked to know more about Honey Buxom.

OUTSIDE, THE SNOW came down fierce and heavy. Blake and the other men had given up on driving the little sedan out of the rut where it had gotten stuck. Using brute force, they dragged the vehicle to the side of the road where it wouldn't get run over by the snowplow.

"If the snowplow gets through," Skip said. "I doubt we're going to see that guy until the snow stops."

Alvardo had his regular cell phone out and was waving it around, trying to get a signal. "Nothing," he muttered. "I'm getting nothing."

Being cut off from his electronic devices was obviously driving him crazy. His identity was completely tied up in his ability to stay connected. Or was it?

As much as Blake tried to analyze each of these men as a threat, he couldn't find anything suspicious. Their cover stories were too good. Ollie and the Dewdrops appeared to be nothing more than a casual indie band, making their own unique brand of guitar and flute music as they traveled around the country. Skip had the earnest, young politician routine down pat. Alvardo was the very definition of military ambition. Maddox was quiet and might deserve a closer look. Ramon Martinez was a wild card because Blake didn't know anything about him other than Sarah said his family had been caterers in the area for a long time.

As the others trudged back toward the house, he pulled Jeremy aside. Blake owed him an explanation. In a low voice, he said, "I lied when I told the others we couldn't find the terminal box."

"I thought so," Jeremy said. "I've never known you to get lost."

"The box was sabotaged with a bullet hole through the center. Somebody wanted to cut off our communication, and I'm thinking it might be an inside job."

Jeremy's gaze lifted to the men walking in front of them. "One of those guys?"

"It's possible. And your dad mentioned terrorists."

Jeremy stopped walking. "Let me see if I've got this right. We might be snowed in with a terrorist who has a vendetta against my father."

"You have another choice," Blake said. "It won't be easy to drive away from here, but it's possible. If you leave right now, you and Emily could make it into town or, at least, to a neighbor's house."

"It's a risk. The snow is coming down pretty

damn hard, and it's ten miles of winding roads to reach an intersection."

"Is it that far? I saw other houses along this road."

"Vacation homes," Jeremy said. "Most of them don't have water in the winter. They're vacant."

"Is it worth the risk?" If he'd been in Jeremy's shoes, he didn't know what he'd decide.

"Can't do it. Even if I knew Emily and I would make it to safety, I can't leave my dad here. They're after him. The terrorists are after him."

Someone wanted to harm the general, to show him he would never be safe. But who?

Chapter Eighteen

In the kitchen, Sarah explained the situation to Slim and his children. "When I first made the catering arrangements, I thought we'd just be feeding the wedding party, the general's aides and the senator's speechwriter, which is ten people. Then the band showed up and I added another three."

"Si, trece," Slim said. "Thirteen."

"But now, the twins and the stripper are staying. So it's sixteen. And, of course, you're going to need to eat."

"We can work it out," Marisol assured her. "If you've got heavy drinkers, we might run short on wine. Otherwise, we'll spread the portions around."

"Feel free to use anything in the pantry," Sarah said.

"We don't like to get into our clients' supplies," Marisol said. "But we might need to, especially if we're snowed in all day tomorrow."

She didn't even want to consider that possibility.

If they were stuck here after Sunday, she'd claw her way out with her bare hands. Pasting on a smile, she turned to Emily, who she was dragging along with her to help with preparations. "Next problem is finding somewhere for everyone to sit. We're going to be really crowded around the dining room table."

"Send the band and the twins into the game room to eat," she said. "I would say to send Honey with them, but the boys will drool all over her food."

"Sounds like a plan."

Together, she and Emily arranged the dining table with her best china, a fragrant white rose centerpiece and several candles. Other candles were scattered around the room, creating a romantic glow as they glistened on the silver. Sarah stepped back and took a look at their handiwork. *Beautiful!* She remembered why they were here: to witness a wedding. Rituals were important, even more so in the presence of danger and threat.

"I'm so happy for you, Emily."

"It's really pretty, isn't it? I'm glad we didn't run off to Vegas."

If this had been a more typical wedding, this fancy dinner would have come after the rehearsal for the ceremony. But they didn't have a justice of the peace, and the ceremony wasn't going to be anything more than Emily and Jeremy stating vows they had written while Ollie and the Dewdrops played in the background. Not much practice was required.

Blake and Jeremy strode into the dining room together. Both wore guns at their hips. Their matching expressions were preoccupied and concerned and aggressively masculine.

"Ladies," Blake said, "is everything under control?"

"I believe so," Sarah answered.

Emily checked her wristwatch. "We have just enough time to dress for dinner."

Sarah didn't want to bother. "I can wear this."

"No way," Emily said. "You had a spa day. Your nails are gorgeous. And you're wearing makeup. You need to dress appropriately for a five-star dinner of crab cakes with a beet salad, beef bourguignon with fresh-made pasta, peas and pearl onions and chocolate mousse dessert."

"Do you think the food will care if I wear jeans?"

"That's fine if you wear a nice top," Emily said. "I think the gray silk."

The two couples went through the front room where the Dewdrops and the stripper were sitting by the fireplace waiting for the feast. Sarah wasn't sure where the others were and wondered how Blake was keeping track of the suspects. Or if he had narrowed the list. While Jeremy escorted

Emily into their room, she went with Blake into hers and closed the door.

As soon as they were alone, he held her and kissed her hard. The muscles in his arms tensed. Her breasts crushed against his hard chest. He held her so tightly that she could hardly take a breath, and she liked his strength. His fierce need matched hers. She wanted him.

All afternoon, she'd been pretending that nothing was wrong, and the strain of holding back her emotions was nearly unbearable. She was angry, furious that they were caught in this situation through no fault of their own. And she was scared, desperate to escape.

She wanted to absorb herself into Blake, to bring him inside her. There wasn't enough time. They should get back to the others, to make sure they didn't kill each other.

Forcibly, she disentangled her arms. Breathing in heavy gasps, she looked up at him. His blue eyes were on fire.

Hoping to lighten the mood, she reached for the tip of his nose. Before she could honk, he grasped her wrist. "Don't," he said. "I don't want to relax. I need to stay alert."

She didn't argue. "What have you learned this afternoon? Who do you suspect?"

"Everybody," he growled. "And nobody."

"Frustrating."

"You're damned right it is." He paced across her bedroom and sank into a chair by the small round table. "I'm inclined to let Ollie and the Dewdrops off the hook. We checked them out before we lost communication, and Kovak ran them through his criminal database. I guess there's a chance that they're using fake identities, but Alvardo has good sources."

"His name comes up a lot," she said. "Alvardo has the internet connections. He keeps track of the threats to the general. He's like a big, fat spider sitting in the middle of his web."

"I'm more suspicious of him than anyone else." He flexed his shoulders and stretched. "Alvardo goes for a run every morning, which would be a time when he could sabotage the terminal or rendezvous with other conspirators. He could be using his internet connections to chat with just about anyone."

"But he's the general's aide, a lieutenant."

"A job he's held for almost a year," Blake said. "And he works at the Pentagon, which means he's gone through some pretty intense security checks himself. If the threat is connected to any known terrorist organization, Alvardo isn't a part of it. I can guarantee that."

"And Maddox?"

"He has two older brothers who served under General Hamilton and credit the general's leadership with saving their lives. Maddox fought to win his position as the general's aide, and he says he'd do anything for him."

"Do you believe him?"

Blake scowled as he considered. "My gut tells me that Maddox is loyal."

"Your gut is good enough for me." She crossed the room, sat on his lap and breathed into his ear. "Do we have time to make love before we join the others?"

"I'd like nothing more." His hand cupped her breast. "Every time I see you, I want you."

"I know." She nipped his earlobe, agilely jumped from his lap and went to her closet. "Getting dressed for dinner seems ridiculous."

"Come on, princess. You like being beautiful."

She didn't change out of her jeans or boots, figuring that if she was sitting at the table nobody would notice the lower half of her body. If she was up and running around, helping serve or fetching more wine, the jeans and boots were appropriate. Inside her closet, she yanked her sweater over her head. The gray silk blouse Emily had suggested flowed over her skin with a subtle whisper. She added a fitted, black velvet jacket for warmth.

She stepped out of the closet and posed for him. "Ta-da!"

"Nice," he said.

She sashayed across the room toward him. "Give me one last kiss before I put on my lipstick."

She heard a loud popping noise.

The lights went out.

IN NEARLY TOTAL darkness, Blake leaped to his feet and reached out for her. The instant his hand made contact with her arm, he pulled her protectively against his chest. His gun was drawn.

"Wait," she said. "Over here on the dresser, there's a flashlight."

He'd noticed the plastic flashlight. "Were you expecting a blackout?"

Taking his hand, she led him across the bedroom and picked up the flashlight, which she immediately turned on. "I thought with the phone lines down, the electricity might go next. I had the twins put flashlights all over the house."

"What's the procedure for when the power goes down?"

"I don't know. It's never happened when I was in charge. We should start in the basement. The fuse box and the generator are down there."

Outside her bedroom, several people were calling out to each other. A flashlight beam appeared from across the hall, and Blake saw Emily and Jeremy.

"Stick with us," Blake said. "Let's get everybody rounded up and settled in the front room near the fireplace."

With Sarah and Emily holding the flashlights, they climbed to the second floor and went down the hall to the general's room. Jeremy knocked, "Dad? Are you in there?"

"We're here," Maddox answered for him. "Is it safe?"

Blake appreciated the caution. "We're gathering everyone in the front room."

The door cracked open and Maddox stepped back, his handgun held at the ready. The general, clad in his uniform with a chest full of ribbons and medals, stepped into the hallway. "What happened?"

Sarah answered, "A power line might have blown down."

"I heard a snapping noise just before the lights went out. Have you checked for fire?"

"I hadn't thought of that," Sarah said. "Blake, we need to get down to the basement right away."

At the other end of the hall, the senator and Rebecca waved flashlights. "What's going on?" Hank asked. "Is everyone all right?"

"Come with us," Emily said.

From downstairs, they heard a huge crash, followed by a shout, a scream and another crash. Moving as quickly as possible, they descended the staircase. The beams of their flashlights showed the shattered remains of the beautifully set dining room table. Skip and one of the Dewdrops stood yelling at each other. It wasn't clear which of them had stumbled first, but Sarah's best china had taken the brunt of their clumsiness.

"Make sure all the candles are out," Sarah ordered as she hurried through the dining room into the kitchen. He followed her into the mudroom and down the staircase into the basement. The pitch darkness in the windowless room was intense. Sarah's thin flashlight beam barely made a difference.

"I don't see a fire." Relief was obvious in her voice. "We need more light down here."

In his rental SUV, he had a heavy-duty, high-beam light, which he should have brought inside before the snow became impassable. "Didn't you say you had camping gear stored down here?"

She turned her beam toward the shelves beyond the laundry area. "I have Coleman lanterns."

Another flashlight beam shone down the staircase. One of the twins called down, "Have you checked the fuse box yet?"

"I need more light," Sarah said. "Would you come down here and help me with these lanterns?"

They carried three lanterns and the container with fuel back up to the kitchen where the Ramirez family was trying to keep cooking with no stove and no burners. Blake left the twin and Sarah in the kitchen to prepare the lanterns and went to the front room where everyone had gathered.

A quick head count showed him that they were two short. In the weird illumination of the flashlights, he saw expressions of excitement, anger and confusion. "We're missing two people—Ollie and Alvardo. Has anyone seen them?"

"Ollie was taking a nap upstairs," said a Dewdrop. "Should I go look for him?"

Blake didn't want to start sending people off on solo missions. "Go with John Reuben and Maddox. Find Ollie and bring him down here. Now, where's Alvardo?"

"I was talking to him," Honey said as she wrapped a multicolored shawl around her neck and shoulders. "Then the lights went off, and I don't know where he went."

They'd have to organize a search. Alvardo could have disappeared due to a perfectly logical reason, like falling and hitting his head. Or Alvardo could be lying in wait, taking advantage of this moment of confusion.

"When the boys get back with Ollie, we'll search. In the meantime, make yourselves as comfortable as possible. We'll try to get the generator working."

Back in the kitchen, he was pleased to see all three lanterns with mantles burning brightly. He gave one to William Reuben. "Take this into the other room. Keep an eye on the people in there and don't let anybody wander off."

"Yes, sir."

"We'll leave another lantern in the kitchen," he said.

"Gracias," Slim said. "We can finish dinner."

Blake gave the third lantern to Sarah and headed back toward the basement. The light flared brightly around them as they descended the staircase and crossed the concrete floor. When he touched her arm, he felt her tremble.

"It's going to be all right," he said.

"You don't know that for sure."

Her fear was natural, and her doubt. "I need for you to be strong."

"I'll do my best."

He remembered how she'd handled their first chase and how she'd managed to climb down the rocks to rescue Franks. If anyone could hold it together in a tense situation, it was Sarah.

The door on the large metal fuse box hung open. Burn marks streaked across the concrete wall. Shards of plastic and metal wires scattered on the floor. From his years in the Middle East, Blake had dealt with a variety of bombs, and he recognized this setup. There had been a small, targeted explosion at the fuse box.

The blackout wasn't a result of the power lines going down. The power had been deliberately sabotaged. Someone wanted them in the dark.

Chapter Nineteen

Sarah was beyond being surprised or shocked by what they'd found. Expecting the unexpected was the order of the day…or the night. The fear and confusion that had been rattling inside her head went silent. She didn't have the luxury of allowing her emotions free rein. "This wasn't an accident."

Blake squatted down and picked through the scrap littered below the metal box. "If I had to guess, I'd say that a small charge was fastened onto the box with a plastic clip. It was detonated from somewhere else in the house."

"Like Franks's backpack," she said. "But how could that be? The cell phones don't work."

"Old-fashioned technology," he said, "like a detonator button."

Anger sparked inside her. They were being manipulated, driven by one circumstance after another toward an unknown end. "Why is this happening? If someone wanted to hurt the general or the senator, why would they wait until they were here in my house? Why would they want to destroy the wedding?"

"It's a message," he said. "The general was right about that."

"Well, I don't get it, and I'm not going to waste time thinking about it." She picked up the lantern and started toward the staircase. "I need both of the Reuben twins in the basement with me to get the generator working."

"Both of them? They're my go-to men for security."

"They grew up in their father's hardware store, and they're good handymen, especially when it comes to emergency repairs. The boys might patch things up with a wad of chewing gum and a roll of duct tape, but it works."

He caught up with her at the foot of the staircase. "Sarah, I appreciate your determination, but I—"

"You should appreciate me," she said. "You should be really glad that I'm not a true princess who sits in the corner and combs her lovely hair. Bottom line—I'm the tough peasant chick who keeps things running."

She had a lot more to say, but he silenced her with a kiss that took her breath away. A shimmer flashed inside her head and eclipsed her angry frustration. All she really wanted was to keep kissing him and holding him. If her problems could just fade away, that would be just fine with her.

He gazed into her eyes. "Like I was saying, you tend to get real determined when you set yourself a goal."

"Do I?"

"Like jumping into a car and refusing to get out."

She recalled that first night when she wouldn't let him boss her around and had ended up witnessing a police takedown. "Are you saying that's a bad thing?"

"I wouldn't have you any other way." He lightly kissed her forehead. "For right now, you need to be careful. Don't go anywhere in the house alone."

"Do I need a weapon?"

He paused to think. "There are already too many guns. Both the Reuben boys are armed. Stick with them."

"Not a problem."

She expected to spend the next couple of hours in the basement trying to get the power back on.

WHEN BLAKE RETURNED to the dining room, he found William Reuben and one of the Dewdrops helping Ollie get settled on the sofa. In the blackout, Ollie had slipped coming down the staircase and sprained his ankle. Alvardo still hadn't been located.

While Rebecca tended to the injured man, Blake pulled Jeremy to one side. Outside the circle of light provided by the lantern, they stood in shadow. He quietly confided, "The fuse box in the basement was purposely blown, and Sarah needs both of the twins to help her get the generator working. You and I have to divvy up the protection and search duty."

Jeremy nodded. They'd worked together so long that he didn't need further explanation. "I'll take protection," he said. "Everybody stays in this room. No exceptions."

"And I'll look for Alvardo." Blake's suspicions about the general's aide appeared to be correct, which meant that everything Alvardo had okayed—including the IDs for the band, the stripper and the caterers—couldn't be counted on. "I'm going to take the senator with me."

"Good idea," Jeremy said. "The last thing I need down here is for those two old guys to get into a scuffle."

"It's likely that your father is the primary target."

"Agreed." His voice tightened. "I'll protect the old man."

Blake gave Jeremy the walkie-talkie the twins had been using so they could stay in touch. Then he stepped into the light from the lantern to address the others. "Listen up, people. Sarah thinks we'll be able to get the power back on. Until then, we're in the dark. I don't want anybody else to get hurt so we'll all stay together in this room."

"We're on the buddy system," Jeremy added. "Nobody goes anywhere without telling me or without taking a buddy."

"What about dinner?" Ollie asked.

"I think we can manage that," Jeremy said. "Emily and Maddox, start cleaning up the mess on the dining table."

Blake said. "Hank, I want you to come with me. We'll try to locate Alvardo."

The senator followed him as he crossed the room to the central staircase. He paused at the front desk to pick up the keys. The first place to search was Alvardo's bedroom. Though both he and the senator had flashlights, navigating through the dark was clumsy. Hank groped along the walls until he stood opposite the desk. "What do you need for me to do?"

"I know your position on gun control, sir. Do you know how to handle a firearm?"

"Yes."

Blake unlocked the front closet where they had been keeping the weapons and found a handgun. He checked the clip and handed it to the senator. "The safety is off."

"If my friends in Congress could see me now, I'd never live it down."

"Keep your eyes open and watch for a threat." Blake climbed the staircase with his gun held at the ready. On the landing, he waited for Hank to catch up. "Are you ready?"

"Why did you choose me to come with you? Any of the younger men would be better at this."

Blake shrugged. "I can trust you. I know you're not working with the bad guys."

"I assume we're considering Alvardo to be a threat," Hank said. "Are we looking for anyone else?"

"I don't know."

"You don't have to worry about what you tell me," he said. "This isn't a political situation, and I have no intention of using any information."

Blake hadn't thought of politics and how the threat might look to a senator. If he mentioned terrorists, would he be hearing his words parroted back on a CNN interview? "Before this night is over, things might come out that cast an unflattering light on the general."

"Charles," he said. "We've been getting along. At least, we haven't ripped into each other."

"I would appreciate…" He paused to rephrase. "I'm sure that your daughter and your future son-in-law would appreciate your discretion."

"I don't hold with secrets. That's how conspiracies get started. Everything needs to be aboveboard."

"Even if it hurts your family?"

The senator didn't answer. Blake listened to the

shuffling of their footsteps as they went down the hallway. Outside Alvardo's room, he turned to the senator. The glow from his flashlight showed a scowl on the older man's face.

"I can't promise to stay silent," Hank said. "If the events at this wedding lead to a greater truth, it's my obligation to speak out."

"Charles is part of your family," Blake reminded him. "You owe him a measure of loyalty."

"This isn't easy for me. I don't want to alienate Emily. She's my only child."

And his life would have been easier if his daughter was getting married to a liberal English professor at Berkeley. But that's not what happened. "Emily fell in love with Jeremy, a good man and a soldier."

"I'm proud of Jeremy and his service to our country," Hank said. "And I respect Charles. Damn it, Blake, I'm not trying to be difficult."

"Was I right to trust you?" It was a serious question. "Do you have my back, Hank?"

"Yes." He straightened his shoulders. "I'll do whatever is necessary to protect the people I love."

"Welcome to the war zone, Senator."

Blake flipped through the keys and opened the door to the bedroom. He'd noticed before that Alvardo was careful to keep his door locked. If they were lucky, they'd find clues here.

After making sure the man wasn't hiding in the

closet or under the bed, he searched the obvious places—the dresser, a drawer in the bedside table, shelves in the closet and Alvardo's suitcase. In the top drawer of a small desk, he found a silver ring, intricately carved with flower designs.

Hank peered over his shoulder. "It's too small for him. Did Alvardo have a girlfriend?"

"Not that I know of." Ironically, the person who had all that detailed background information about the people in the house was Alvardo himself.

"A wedding ring?"

"There's an inscription inside." Blake held the flashlight so he could see the carved letters. "It's in Arabic. It says 'My Beloved Daughter, Salima.'"

"Not a wedding ring."

"Muslims don't usually exchange rings," Blake said. "But there are gifts of jewelry for the bride. Like this ring."

Alvardo had suggested a terrorist connection to the general. If the ring was evidence of that plot, why had he hidden it in his desk drawer? Instead of finding answers in this search, he was turning up more questions. Alvardo had more secrets than anyone knew.

Under the pillow on the neatly made bed, Hank found a Glock, which he handed over to Blake. The gun was loaded, ready to go.

"This isn't right," Blake said. "The reason for sleeping with a gun under your head is to be ready to react and protect yourself. If Alvardo is an assassin, why would he be worried about somebody sneaking up on him?"

"Maybe he didn't trust the people he was working with," Hank suggested.

That suggested other attackers, outside the house. But the charge that sabotaged the fuse box had been planted by someone on the inside. Had Alvardo turned out the lights? Why?

Blake grabbed the briefcase that Alvardo took with him everywhere. Inside were folders, envelopes and reports. He passed it to Hank. "Hold on to this. The material in here could become evidence."

Hank frowned. "Charles won't be happy to see me with all his personal correspondence in hand."

"When we go downstairs, you can hand it over to him. It'd be a nice gesture, a show of trust."

"You're more of a politician than you think, Blake."

IN THE BASEMENT, Sarah decided that the best way she could help was to assign herself to guard duty, leaving the twins free to work their magic. She paced behind them, holding the handgun and moving the lantern when they needed to see.

Their first plan had been to get the generator hooked up, but they'd found enough fuses and parts in her toolbox to think they might repair the main fuse box.

"I want this done fast," she reminded them.

"That's how we do it," John said.

William added, "Our dad always says, 'Do you want it done fast or do you want it done right?' We tell him, 'Both.'"

From where she stood, she had an unobstructed view from one end of the basement to the other where it faded into darkness, and she was glad that she never allowed this area to become a repository for broken furniture and other junk. At one time, she'd considered making part of the basement into a wine cellar, but those plans had faded along with the economy.

John twisted a screw and sparks shot out from the box. He guffawed. "I guess that wasn't the right place."

"Are you all right?" she asked.

"It takes more than electrocution to keep me down."

"Seriously," she said, "is it safe for you to be working on this?"

William answered, "Don't worry. Most of the cabins around here have ancient electricity that has to be twisted and tweaked. We can figure it out."

As she watched, ten minutes passed as slowly as ten hours. Her gaze lifted to the ceiling, and she wished she could see through the floor and know what was going on in the main part of the house. Had they located Alvardo? Was the food being served? And where was Blake? She imagined him prowling through the halls, gun in hand and ready for action.

She looked back at the twins and asked, "Are you guys getting hungry?"

"Oh, yeah."

Silly question. The twins were always hungry. "I'll run upstairs and get a couple of plates of food."

"Wait," William said, "nobody is supposed to go anywhere by themselves."

She wasn't talking about wandering around. "Just up to the kitchen, and I'll be right back."

William hitched up his jeans and came toward her. "I'll go with you."

"Then you leave John down here all alone." She started walking toward the staircase. "Here's the deal. You come over here to the edge of the stairs. Then you can keep an eye on me and your brother at the same time."

Without waiting for an answer, she aimed her flashlight beam on the staircase and rushed up. After the oppressive dark of the basement, it almost felt light in the mudroom. Through the window in the door to the kitchen, the glow of a lantern spilled across the floorboards.

She looked toward the storage bin for firewood.

Blake had been busy, probably too busy to worry about tending the fire. She could grab a couple of logs on her way.

Holding the flashlight in one hand, she lifted the lid with the other.

Alvardo stared up at her with sightless eyes. A knife had been buried up to the hilt in his chest. His white sweater was soaked with blood.

Chapter Twenty

Sarah's first reaction was a trained reflex, learned from the first aid and mountain rescue classes she'd taken. Her fingers went to his throat to feel for a pulse. His cold, damp flesh repulsed her, but she kept feeling. Her heart pounded so furiously that, for a moment, she thought she felt a response from Alvardo. She pressed harder, hoping against the inevitable that he was still alive. The logs underneath him shifted, and his body moved along with them.

She yanked her hand away. She wanted to run, but her feet rooted to the floor. A roaring inside her head grew louder and louder, threatened to overwhelm her consciousness. Her knees trembled. She was about to collapse.

"Sarah?" William Reuben called to her. "Are you okay?"

She lowered the lid on the storage bin, not wanting to expose William to this horrible death. "Come up here. I need you."

Standing at the top of the staircase, William shined his flashlight at her. "What's wrong?"

She held up her hand to deflect the beam. The light distracted her and fed into her confusion. Her usual decisive attitude was gone. Truly, she didn't know what to do. "Stay with me, William. I need to think."

There was nothing she could do for Alvardo. He was already gone. If she told the others that he'd been murdered, she didn't know what would happen. Blake had said that he didn't want to force the hand of the person who had been threatening them—the murderer.

Clumsily, William patted her shoulder. "I can tell you're upset. It's going to be okay."

His unknowing reassurances helped. Somehow, everything would be okay. She had to believe that. "I need to talk to Blake. Do you know how I can find him?"

"He and Jeremy have the walkie-talkies. If anybody knows where Blake is, it's Jeremy."

And Jeremy was in the front room with everybody else. Seeing him meant seeing all of them. Knowing that one of them was a murderer, how could she be in the same room with them? She shuddered, remembering the feel of the cold skin at Alvardo's throat. *Hold yourself together. Be strong.* She gasped, trying to catch her breath. Her chin lifted and her backbone stiffened. "I want you to come with me, William. Then we need to send someone down to the basement to guard your brother while he works on the box."

"Maddox," William said. "He's been hanging around with us for a couple of days, and he's a good guy."

"Yes, Maddox."

She lurched forward, concentrating on each step so she wouldn't topple and fall. She made it through the kitchen, responding to questions from Slim Ramirez without really knowing what she'd said.

In the front room, she found Jeremy keeping watch as most of the crowd sat around the dining room table and ate the elegantly prepared food off paper plates. Their conversations were quiet, and the occasional laughter had a nervous edge. Ollie was stretched out on the sofa with his injured leg elevated on pillows.

She clutched Jeremy's arm and pulled him off to one side. "I need to talk to Blake. Where is he?"

"What's wrong?" he asked. "I can help."

In her mind, there was only one possible course of action. She needed Blake. "Please, just tell me."

"He's searching the whole house. Right now, he's on the third floor in the dormitory area."

William stepped up and did her talking for her. "I'm going to take Sarah up there. She wanted you to send Maddox down to the basement to keep an eye on my brother. Is that okay?"

"I'll take care of it," Jeremy said. "How's the repair going?"

"Pretty good," William said. "My brother is good at rigging stuff together."

She looked toward the central staircase. Now that she knew where Blake was, she was anxious to find him. Jeremy caught hold of her arm. "Is that blood on your sleeve?"

"I cut myself while I was helping with the repairs," she lied. "No big deal."

With William accompanying her, she went to the staircase and began to climb. The more she moved, the better she felt. She hadn't recovered from the shock of finding the body.... She might never recover. But she was no longer on the verge of fainting.

At the top of the stairs on the third floor, Blake and Hank were waiting for them with flashlights aimed in their direction.

"You promised to stay put," Blake growled.

"I couldn't."

"Sarah, you have to be careful."

She stumbled into his arms and clung to him. The floodgates burst and she sobbed into his shoulder. Sarah held nothing back. Her body heaved and trembled with each deep moan. Tears poured down her cheeks.

Unable to maintain the strength to stand, she slipped down his body toward the floor. Blake caught her under the armpits and carried her to one of the dormitory-style beds. When he lay her down, she reached for him. "Don't leave me."

Sitting on the bed beside her, he held her against him. "Tell me what happened, princess."

Looking past his shoulder, she saw the worried faces of William and Hank. Could she share this information with them? Was she making a mistake? It didn't matter. She was here with Blake, and she believed in him. He would make this right.

"Alvardo," she said. "He's dead, murdered. I found his body in the wood bin in the mudroom."

Her head ached from the tears and the sobs, but it felt good to talk. She needed to tell him everything that she could remember. "He was stabbed in the chest with a hunting knife, I think. The hilt is sticking out. He has on a white sweater and it's covered in blood. His eyes…his eyes are open."

"Did you tell anyone else?" Blake asked.

"No, I came right here."

"You did the right thing, Sarah."

She inhaled the first real breath since finding the body. Leaning against Blake's broad chest, she waited for her mind to clear.

BLAKE WISHED HE had as much faith in himself as Sarah had in him. He'd been thinking of Alvardo as the threat. Instead, he was a victim. And there was a murderer loose in the house with them.

Though he continued to hold Sarah, he was talking to Hank and William. "We need to be careful. The murderer is capable of killing without mercy. If we set him off, he might attack. More people would be hurt."

"Who do you think it is?" William asked.

"Let's take a look at the facts," Hank said. The calm tone of his voice told Blake that this was a man accustomed to dealing with crisis. "Alvardo must have been killed during the blackout. I'd guess that there were five to seven minutes of confusion when everybody was running around like chickens with their heads cut off. His body was found in the mudroom, which is outside the kitchen."

"The caterers were in the kitchen," William said. "They were close by. It could be one of them."

"Or else," Hank said, "Alvardo might have arranged to meet the killer in that particular place."

Blake liked the way their logic was playing out. "We can eliminate a couple of suspects. Maddox immediately went to the general's room to protect him. That clears both of them."

"That's good," William said, "because Maddox is in the basement alone with my brother."

Blake summarized, "That leaves the other two musicians, the caterers, Skip Waverly-Smythe and

Honey Buxom. Hank, what can you tell us about your speechwriter?"

"He comes from a wealthy family in Los Angeles. They're old money, commercial real estate. Skip has a master's degree in journalism from Stanford. He tried investigative reporting but preferred writing opinion pieces."

"Was he in the Middle East?" Blake asked, thinking of the ring they'd found in Alvardo's room. *My Beloved Daughter, Salima.* He had a feeling that when they found out about Salima, they would know their killer.

"Skip was embedded in Iraq," Hank said. "He's been on my team for almost a year. For what it's worth, I never would have suspected him of committing a violent crime."

Blake needed more information from Sarah. Lightly, he stroked her hair. "How are you feeling? Can you talk?"

"Much better," she said.

"I have a couple of questions for you, and I want you to think before you answer." Her breathing had returned to a normal level, but he didn't want to get her worked up again. "You said he was stabbed in the chest. Was there much blood?"

"A huge stain on the front of his sweater."

"Stabbed more than once?"

She shook her head. "I couldn't say for sure, but I don't think so."

A single puncture wound leaving the weapon in place limited the blood splatter. Slicing wounds were messy. The killer would have been covered in blood.

"Could you tell how Alvardo got into the wood bin? Was he dragged across the floor? Or carried?"

"I didn't see a blood trail but—like you said—the light wasn't good." She paused for a moment to think. "I suppose, if he was leaning back against the bin, the killer could have flipped open the lid and pushed him over the edge."

That was the information Blake wanted. Carrying the body would have limited the suspects to men. But if Alvardo was shoved, a woman could have done it. The ridiculously named Honey Buxom could be their murderer.

Hank cleared his throat. "I don't like the way this is working out. I need to be downstairs with my wife and daughter."

"Can you go back down there and not say anything?"

He nodded vigorously. "I don't like secrets, Blake, but I get it. There are times when it's necessary to conceal information."

The senator had an interesting set of ethics, one that bended to suit his needs. Not that Blake was any better. Sometimes you had to lie to reach the greater truth.

"Here's how this is going to work," Blake said.

"You and William go downstairs and blend in with the others, don't raise any alarms. I want to take a few more minutes with Sarah until she's feeling better, then we'll join you."

"Maybe we should put Sarah in her room to sleep," Hank suggested.

"Nobody goes anywhere alone." That was how people got picked off. "We stay in a group. Or go with a buddy."

"Fine," Hank said. "What next?"

"When I come downstairs, I want to put our suspects into different rooms, supposedly for questioning. The Ramirez family goes in one room. The musicians in another. Then Honey. Then Skip. The murderer will slip up. It might be blood on their clothes. Or an inability to account for those minutes in the blackout." When he had the suspects alone, he intended to show them the ring. "We'll take the killer into custody. Nobody gets hurt."

As if to emphasize the simple clarity of his plan, the lights came back on. Without a slight flicker, the overhead track lighting that ran the length of the dormitory brightly illuminated the row of single beds along one wall.

Electricity felt like a miracle. Finally, things were going their way.

William gave a whoop. "I knew John could do it."

"He's a genius," Blake said.

"He's MacGyver," said Sarah as she applauded. "John fixed the fuse box using a minimum of equipment and supplies."

She was already looking better. When she'd first stumbled into the room with her skin as white as parchment and her dark eyes looking like she'd faced the demons of hell, he'd been scared for her. Seeing the victim of violent death changed a person. He still remembered his first time, the day he'd engaged in battle and lost his innocence.

When Hank and William left, he hugged her close. "I'm sorry this happened to you."

"Me, too." Her arms weren't as strong as usual, but she managed to hug him back. "All I kept thinking was that I had to find you. You'd make everything all right."

"I want you to keep thinking that. Never stop trusting me." He gave her a small grin. "Maybe, someday, you'll actually listen when I tell you to do something."

"Probably not."

There was more he needed to say. They'd only known each other for a brief time, but he had deep feelings for this woman. He might even love her. "I'd like to have the chance to find out how well we fit together."

"Are you talking about that trip to New Orleans?"

"Maybe," he said. "After I'm done with my final

deployment in about six months, I want to come back here."

"For a visit?"

"I'd come for a longer stay than that. I think mountain rescue would be a good second career for me. It's active. I'm helping people. And I'm not stuck behind a desk."

"And you want to stay here with me while you're training?"

He gazed directly into her strong yet delicate face. "Are you trying to make this hard for me?"

"I'm being specific." She pushed her hair off her forehead and smiled. "If I want a clear definition, I need to ask questions, lots of questions. I know you're not proposing a long-term commitment. We're both too grown-up to make that kind of leap without looking."

"You're right." But he felt like leaping. He wanted to tell her that he loved her. Too soon, it was way too soon.

"But there's a bond between us. I can't explain it."

"We'll have time to figure it out," he said. "I'd like to book a room for the next two weeks."

"I'll have to check my reservation book."

"Actually, I'd like to book *your* bedroom. The space beside you on *your* bed."

She leaned forward and gave him a peck on the cheek. "I've been saving the space for you."

"That's what I was waiting to hear."

She wiggled around on the bed until her legs were dangling over the side. "All that crying took a lot out of me. I've never sobbed like that before."

He slung an arm around her slender shoulders. "It's okay."

"I should get up and move around before we go downstairs and put your plan into effect. I want to get this over with before anyone else gets hurt."

Holding his hand, she slowly walked the length of the room and back again. He could feel her strength and her confidence returning.

Abruptly, she came to a halt. Her eyes widened as she stared at an object that was partially tucked behind the head of one of the beds. "Is that what I think it is?"

He looked past her and saw the seemingly innocent object. Something that could be purchased in any department store. He knew exactly what it was. The design and color matched the backpack Franks had been carrying—the backpack filled with explosives.

Chapter Twenty-One

Sarah's mind was working well enough for her to know that they were in mortal danger. The murderer who set the charge in the basement fuse box was up to the same trick with the backpack. Blake was already pulling her toward the staircase and away from the bomb.

"Stop." She dug in her heels. "We've found it in time. We can get rid of the damn thing before it does any damage."

"That's a risk I'm not willing to take. Having the lights back on might spook the killer. He might be anxious to make his next move."

"He or she," she said absently. Her gaze remained focused on the backpack. "If it explodes up here, it's going to tear off a chunk of the roof. Do you know how expensive that is to repair?"

"I'll pay for it," he offered. "Sarah, this is one of those times when you need to listen to me. I know about explosives. I know what I'm talking about."

"But this is my home. I can't let it be destroyed."

"What's more important? Your B and B or your life?"

She shouldn't have hesitated for a moment, but she did. Bentley's had been in her family forever, she'd grown up here and she loved the place. The house had been the center of her world for a very long time. "My life, of course."

"You're never going to leave this place, are you?"

"Why would I?"

"What if I asked you to move away with me?"

This wasn't the time for a discussion about whether he was more important than her home. Time was passing. She needed to take advantage of this chance to save her home.

She went to one of the dormer windows that poked out from the side of the roof. On the third floor, she hadn't replaced the old windows with the triple-pane glass she'd used in the rest of the house to keep in the warmth. The dormitory was always warm. In summer, it was hot, and she'd kept the old windows that fastened with a latch in the center and could be easily opened to let the fresh breezes in.

Turning the center window latch required a bit of strength but she got it open and pulled the windows inside. There was a storm window that fastened on with screws, but she figured she could knock it out with the flat of her hand. She aimed for a screw on the left side and gave a hard smack. The storm window shuddered in its frame but didn't budge. She hit again and again. Nothing moved. Outside the snow had piled high the window sill.

Blake stood beside her. "What the hell are you doing?"

"If I get the storm window out of the way, I can throw the backpack out the window."

"I'll do it."

As he punched at the side rails of the storm window, she looked down at the backpack. It wasn't making a ticking noise or showing a digital countdown, but she felt the urgency. Could this decision cost her life? "Hurry, Blake."

He grabbed a wooden chair from behind one of the small desks and used the legs to batter the window. The glass shattered. Snow drifted over the sill and onto the floor. The storm burst inside with all its fury.

She passed him the backpack. Leaning over the sill, he swung the pack by one of the straps and flung it as far as he could away from the house.

He pulled back inside. With a struggle, he closed the window and fastened the center latch. It wasn't fastened tightly; she could feel the cold air rushing through, but she'd fix the window later. She went toward him for a hug.

He held her off. "You can't always have everything your way, Sarah. There has to be give-and-take."

"Why are you angry?"

"You just risked your life—and mine, as well—because you didn't want your precious house to be damaged. You won't compromise."

"But everything worked out."

"We're not talking about end results. It's the process." There was a deep, resonant, serious tone to his voice. "I don't have much experience with relationships. My life is changing. I'm thinking about settling down. Everything is different, and it seems like I'm taking all the risks while you sit on your throne and refuse to meet me halfway."

"On my throne?" She hated the princess accusation. "You're not mad at me, Blake. You're mad at yourself. You say you want to settle down. Is that really what you're after?"

"Yes."

His blue eyes were hard and unyielding. It occurred to her that she needed to tread lightly. She might lose him. "I don't want it to be like this."

"You could change," he suggested.

"What if I don't want to change?"

"I'm glad I found out now," he said. "Without compromise, we haven't got a chance."

She'd heard this song and dance before. It was what men said before they left her. They couldn't stand being around a strong woman. Or was she just a stubborn woman? There was a possibility that she was using her tough girl facade to protect herself. Vulnerability sucked, but she didn't want to make a mistake with him. In just a few days, he had become too important to her. She needed to say something, but her mouth was frozen.

"Let's go downstairs," he said. "I want to get this over with."

"Fine with me."

When Sarah turned toward the staircase, she saw her way was blocked by Honey Buxom. In her graceful hand, the belly dancer held an automatic handgun. She arched an eyebrow. "Lover's spat?"

"Nobody has used the *L* word," Sarah said. With her emotions roiling, it took a moment to realize that she should be scared. Honey was the killer.

"You threw my property out the window," Honey said, "and that is very inconvenient."

"Are there other explosives planted in the house?" Blake asked.

"No. We've reached the endgame more quickly than I expected. Did you find the body?"

"Yes," Sarah said.

"I suspected as much. When the senator joined our little group downstairs, I could tell that something was wrong. He hugged his wife a little too long and gazed at his daughter with too much fondness. When he took this gun out of his belt and set it on the table, I picked it up and slipped away."

"You came to the third floor to get the bomb," Blake said. "What were you going to do with it?"

"Figure it out. You military men are so clever." She gestured with the barrel of her gun. "Hold your gun by two fingers and toss it over toward me. Don't try anything or I will shoot Sarah."

Blake did as she asked. "What's your real name?"

"Why do you want to know?"

"It's humiliating to be taken down by a stripper named Honey Buxom."

"Halia," she said. "I'm Afghani. Not a soldier or a terrorist, just a citizen."

"Hard to believe," Blake said. "Franks was scared of you."

"He's a rabbit, afraid of his own shadow." She undulated toward them—dangerous in a beautiful, sensual way. "And Franks had dealings with one of my uncles, a gunrunner. That has nothing to do with me. I'm merely a woman with a broken heart and a broken life."

Sarah might have been sympathetic if Halia hadn't been holding a gun on them and hadn't stabbed Alvardo in the chest. "I have a question," she said. "Why?"

"The wedding, of course."

Blake shook his head. "I'm going to need more than that."

Halia came toward them, picking up Blake's

handgun on the way and tucking it into the waistband of her jeans. She went to the window they'd broken and looked out. "The storm hasn't let up. I suppose we have time to talk."

She posed before the window as though she was performing a special show just for them. Sarah had known crazy people before but no one compared with this woman. Halia was disconnected from reality, dancing in her own strange world.

She spoke in a musical voice. "General Hamilton ordered a strike on my village. It was the day my cousin, Salima, was getting married. She and her groom and three others in my family were killed. My mother and father were already gone. I had no one left but distant uncles. I would have died if I had not been blessed with sizable personal wealth."

"A princess," Sarah said. "I should have known."

"I swore revenge," Halia said, "and I was clever. I cultivated many friendships with Americans, including Lieutenant Alvardo. I think, perhaps, that he fell in love with me."

And she'd paid him back with a knife in the chest. Sarah swallowed her revulsion. She wanted to keep Halia talking until they found a way to disarm her. "You used him."

"In so many ways," Halia said. "He put me in touch with someone who could arrange for my student visa to attend the University of Denver in International Studies. He thought he would turn me into an American girl, but I never forgot my burning hatred for the general. When I heard about the wedding, my mind was made up. I would destroy his son's wedding, and leave the general alive to mourn for the rest of his miserable life."

"That's why you wanted to kidnap Emily," Sarah said. "To hurt General Hamilton."

"That would have been simple. I could have used her to lure her foolish fiancé and killed them both. When Franks failed in that attempt, I provided him with the explosive for another attack. Another failure." Her dark eyes flashed with a light that was both beautiful and dangerous as she stared at Blake. "I was watching you the whole time, keeping my own surveillance away from your cameras."

"Did Alvardo know your plan?" Blake asked.

"Of course not. He knew I was in the area and he called me every morning on his run. When he told me that he'd been put in charge of hiring a stripper for the bachelor party, I saw my way in."

Sarah remembered their spa treatments and Halia's demonstration of belly dancing. "Why did you and Alvardo keep up the ruse?"

"I convinced him that it would be fun. I would perform and then introduce myself to the general, who was a well-known figure in my country. Alvardo was happy to see me. He said he had a gift for me, and he expected me to display the gracious manners of my people."

"But that wasn't your plan."

"I had to cut off communications and destroy the sat phone terminal," she said. "Alvardo guessed my true intention when I sabotaged the fuses and caused the blackout. He confronted me."

"And you killed him," Blake said.

She bared her teeth in a cruel smile. "He didn't understand that revenge requires blood."

"Speaking of blood," Blake said, "how did you keep from getting his blood on your clothes?"

"I changed and left the bloodstained clothes in my room." With the gun, she gestured to the overhead lights. "Now that we're no longer in the dark, you would have found me out quickly. I don't have much time left."

"Surrender your weapon," Blake said, "and we might be able to work out a deal."

"In an American prison?"

"The explosive is gone, Halia. Your plan failed."

"You underestimate me." She shot a glance toward Sarah. "They never think a woman is capable of taking revenge."

"You've made your point," Sarah said. "There's no reason to continue. You're going to get hurt."

"Nothing could hurt more than losing my family, the people I love." Her full lips peeled back in a sneer. "Use the walkie-talkie. Tell Jeremy and Emily to come up here. Tell them to come alone."

"There's something else you should know," Blake said. "Alvardo would have wanted you to know."

"What?"

"This is the gift he brought for you." Blake reached into his pocket and took out a silver ring. "It's inscribed to 'My Beloved Daughter, Salima.'"

"My cousin!" Halia darted toward him, then stepped back against the window. "You think you'll trick me to come closer. No, you won't. Put the ring on the floor."

He hunkered down on the floor, set the ring on the hardwood surface and pushed it toward her. When Halia bent down to pick it up, Blake launched himself toward her. His shoulder connected with her upper chest, driving her backward. Together, they crashed against the window with the poorly fastened latch.

The window flung open. Blake's forward momentum thrust them both through the opening. Halia went all the way out. Blake hung halfway over the window ledge.

With a cry, Sarah ran to help. The storm buffeted them. In seconds, they were wet. Halia had twisted around. She clung desperately to Blake's arm and scrambled to find a foothold on the roof.

Sarah reached for Halia's other flailing arm. Bits of broken glass scratched through her clothes.

When Halia caught her hand, Sarah turned to Blake. "What do we do?"

"We could let go and wave goodbye as she slides down from the roof," he said. "Or we could pull her inside and use her scarves as handcuffs. I'm guessing that Alvardo would want us to save her. I'll bet he had some info on her in those files he was always carrying around."

"Pull," she said.

Together, they hauled Halia over the sill and into the room. When Blake tied her wrists behind her back, Sarah noticed that she was wearing the silver ring that had belonged to her cousin.

Blake used the walkie-talkie to call Jeremy and the twins. When they arrived and took over with Halia, he offered a brief explanation and guided her down the staircase to the first floor. She whisked him down the hallway to her bedroom and closed the door.

"That was close," she said.

"Let's not do it again."

This wasn't the best time to talk about their relationship, but there was something she had to tell him that couldn't wait. "I can change," she said. "I might be bullheaded, but I promise that I'm capable of change."

"I don't want to force you."

"And I don't want you to think it'll be easy. I won't jump through hoops for you, but I will compromise."

He slipped his arm around her. "Prove it."

Gazing into his deep blue eyes, she opened herself up. "I love you, Blake."

The words hung between them for a long moment before he kissed her forehead and whispered, "I love you, my princess."

TWO WEEKS LATER on a white sand beach in Hawaii, Blake performed the ceremony for the delayed wedding of Jeremy Hamilton and Emily Layton. The whole family—including the senator and the general—met as friends.

"I now pronounce you husband and wife," Blake intoned. "Kiss her."

There were cheers all around while Ollie and the Dewdrops played a new original piece about being snowed in with no escape.

After Jeremy had kissed the bride, Sarah walked along the edge of the waves with Blake. They'd been in Hawaii for three days, which seemed to be long enough for her to stop worrying about the B and B. She'd left it in the capable hands of her friend Carrie and the twins.

They stood with their toes in the water, watching the rippling reflection of the Pacific sunset.

She looked up at him and grinned. “Thanks for making me come here.”

“Compromise can be fun,” he said.

“Not too many changes and not too fast.”

They hadn’t been apart since the day they met, and she wasn’t sure how she was going to handle his deployment. He was scheduled to leave in two days and would be gone for nearly six months.

He took her hand and raised it to his lips, brushing a kiss across her knuckles before he dropped to one knee. Her eyes misted with tears when he opened the small black velvet box and showed her a big, sparkling blue diamond.

“Your decision,” he said.

She loved him, loved that he wasn’t afraid to be vulnerable. Taking the ring, she slipped it on her finger. Under her breath, she whispered, “And the princess lived happily ever after…”

* * * * *